Carly Phillips

Brazen

ISBN 0-373-77080-4

BRAZEN

Printed in U.S.A.

PRAISE FOR THE NOVELS
OF CARLY PHILLIPS

New York Times bestseller *HOT STUFF*

"This breezy book will likely score a touchdown
with readers looking for sexy thrills
and instant gratification."
—*Publishers Weekly*

"The romance is hot and spicy but it is Ms. Phillips's
lovely characterization that makes *Hot Stuff*
a savory treat to be read more than once."
—*Rendezvous*

"This first book in The Hot Zone trilogy shines
with Phillips's trademark sizzle and sensuality."
—*Romantic Times* (4 stars)

THE HEARTBREAKER

"Carly Phillips, publishing's newest,
brightest star, shines!"
—Fern Michaels, *New York Times* bestselling author

"A steamy…read."
—*People* magazine

"A perfect 10. Witty, fresh and entertaining."
—*Romance Reviews Today*

THE BACHELOR

"A titillating read… On a scale of 1–5: a high five
for fun, ease of reading and sex. Actually I would've
given it a 6 for sex if I could have."
—Kelly Ripa

"A romantic romp…the sexual chemistry explodes."
—*Publishers Weekly*

"A bubbly romance."
—*Newsday*

Dear Reader,

Thanks to HQN I am so excited to bring you the reissue of my very first Harlequin Temptation novel, *Brazen*. I can still remember the excitement of making that first sale to Harlequin and the joy of receiving fan letters telling me how much readers enjoyed Sam and Mac's story. I have to admit that after all these years I am still partial to these characters. I hope you will love them as much as I do! You can visit my Web site at www.carlyphillips.com to see the original Harlequin Temptation cover as well as all the fantastic reviews, or if you would just like to get in touch with me, you can e-mail me at carly@carlyphillips.com or write to me at P.O. Box 483, Purchase, NY 10577.

Happy reading!

Best wishes,

Carly Phillips

To my husband, Phillip, and my girls, Jaclyn and Jennifer, for all the love and encouragement you give me. And to Mom and Dad for your constant love and support. I couldn't have done it without all of you.

Thanks to Kathy Attalla for reading,
rereading and never letting me give up.
And an extra-special thank-you to my editor,
Brenda Chin, for believing in me from the beginning.

CHAPTER ONE

THE CAR WAS DEAD. Samantha Reed climbed out of what the rental company had called their best midsize luxury vehicle without bothering to try the ignition one last time. That final grinding sound had made things perfectly clear. Although she disliked abandoning the car in the desert, she had no choice. Reliable Rentals would just have to send a tow truck for their useless automobile. Too bad no one would be sending a search-and-rescue squad for the driver, she thought.

Drawing in a deep breath of dry air combined with dust, she took one last look behind her. The vehicle looked an awful lot more comfortable than she felt at the moment, but it obviously had no intention of moving any time soon. She had no choice. The Arizona sun had begun dipping below the distant mountains, and if she waited around much longer, she'd be hiking in the dark. Not that she wanted to hike at all. She certainly wasn't dressed for a jaunt through the desert.

What was that saying about the best-laid plans? She grabbed her purse, left her luggage and gave

one last tug on the hem of her newly acquired tiered
silk skirt. A skirt she'd bought for its coolness and
comfort in the dry desert heat. Of course, she hadn't
counted on a prolonged excursion while wearing it.
This outfit had been a mistake. She hoped she
wouldn't say the same for the upcoming week.

If all she had to look forward to was a marriage as
dry as this godforsaken desert, she intended to cram
a lifetime's worth of fun, lust, passion and excitement
into the time she had left. Next weekend, she'd meet
her fiancé at a seminar on risk management and financial gain at one of Arizona's exclusive resorts, but
first she'd take some calculated risks of her own. She
deserved that much, considering she was sacrificing
her life, giving up her future happiness, for her father.
Years of compliance and acting like the obedient
daughter had brought her to this, to the brink of marriage to a man she didn't love. A man nearly fifteen
years her senior. A man she scarcely knew.

She got out of the car, wobbled on the heels of her
seventies-style shoes and was forced to smooth down
her layered miniskirt once more. There may not be another car in sight, but she'd be damned if she'd moon
the Arizona wildlife. She glanced over her shoulder
at the wide expanse of emptiness behind her. It
couldn't be any worse than what her future held.

In one month, she'd kiss her dreams of happily ever
after goodbye. But she wanted—no, she needed—

some memories to keep her warm on the cold nights ahead. She would never experience what her parents had shared, an all-encompassing love...even to the exclusion of their only daughter. But she could experience passion before she gave up her life on the marital altar. Only now, when it was too late to change things, did Samantha realize she'd spent the past twenty-nine years on a mission—to please her parents and win their love. A futile exercise. They loved her in their own way. It just hadn't been enough for Samantha. And in her search for more, she'd given everything she had in return.

When she'd promised her dying mother that she'd look out for her father, she'd been drawn into her family circle for the first time. Her mother had reached out to her, and she'd given her word freely and unconditionally. She just hadn't counted on how much one promise would change her life. Her stockbroker father had hit a downward turn. As a grieving widower, he'd begun to neglect his business, then to compensate, he'd advised risky ventures for his clients in the hopes of quick gain before he lost their business for good. Things hadn't panned out. To make matters worse, he'd invested personal capital as well. He'd spiraled into debt so deep it threatened his future. And because Samantha had it in her power to fix things, she would.

Tom, her new boss, courtesy of a business buyout, and her father's country club friend, had offered a solution. More like a bribe, Samantha thought. Marriage to Tom would enable her father to pay his creditors, the IRS being the main one, without having to declare bankruptcy. Whether he was capable of starting over again was another question entirely. She'd offered him her savings, but even a financial planner who made more than a decent living couldn't put a dent in his delinquent debts. Not so for a man who bought and sold companies on a whim. Tom's *offer* had been hard to turn down.

She might not care if the Reeds were the laughingstock of the country club set, but her father would. He had little left, and the club provided his only outlet for socialization since her mother's death. Without it, he'd retreat, living in seclusion and depression. Samantha didn't call that living, and she wouldn't place her already-lonely father in such a position. Not if she could help it. And as Tom, the wealthy wheeler-dealer had informed her, she could.

He'd provide enough money to bail out her father in exchange for a wife, a hostess and a trophy on his arm. Any good-looking woman would fill those needs, but Samantha possessed one extra quality. She understood his business and knew how to deal with both his clients and his competitors. She saved him the time and effort of dating and disqualifying the empty-headed women who lined up to be the wife of a rich entrepreneur. His words, not hers.

With her last hours of freedom flying by, her dreams had come down to a hastily conceived plan to indulge in an erotic interlude with a sexy stranger. She'd even dipped into her savings to help the cause. She'd splurged on everything, including the rental car that lay still behind her. She shot the vehicle a disgusted look. If she wanted to have a no-strings, purely sensual affair with the most desirable man she could find, she had to reach her destination first.

Shielding her eyes with her hand, she glanced down the long stretch of highway. If she could even call Bloody Basin Road a highway to begin with. She'd driven south on a road named Golden Guts after leaving the rental place outside the airport and decided she preferred New York State's numerical monikers to the grizzly images conjured up out West. Which way now, she wondered. If she remembered correctly, there had been a ranch-style establishment back a mile or so....

A slight breeze picked up as she lost track of the sun. Goose bumps prickled on her bare arms, legs and back, and she shivered. Lengthening her stride, she trudged on, forcing down the swell of regret and guilt that threatened each time she thought about her plan. Once she married Tom, she'd be the faithful wife he expected, but she wasn't married yet. This week would have to substitute for the honeymoon she'd never have.

Some beginning she'd made. Frustrated with the slow pace and afraid she'd twist an ankle, fall on the side of the highway and be mistaken for roadkill, she pulled off her shoes before continuing. The pace picked up and so did the pain. Small rocks lodged in the soles of her feet as she walked.

By the time she saw lights in the distance, darkness had fallen. Her feet were raw, her throat parched and tears probably stained her cheeks. *Desperate* didn't begin to cover how she was feeling. At this point, she'd give her body to the first man who offered her a place to sit, a shoulder to cry on and a cold drink. Not necessarily in that order.

"HEY, MAC, SLUMMING AGAIN?"

Ryan Mackenzie wiped down the glass top of the old wooden bar with a damp rag. "You know I can't stay away from here," he told the table of old men who frequented The Hungry Bear.

"I can't believe you'd prefer this joint to that fancy spa you own."

Mac glanced at the scarred paneled walls, the crooked pictures, the pool table in the corner and the dartboard in the back. He inhaled and smelled a mixture of nachos, tobacco and beer. "Believe it."

"Give him a break," the tallest of the men said to his friends. "He might have money now, but a boy don't lose his roots."

"And mine are embedded in the same land as you, Zee." Mac recalled the small ranch-style house he'd grown up in and the almost identical house next door. He and his sister, Kate, had been just as comfortable in either one, due mainly to the warmth and humor of the older man in the corner.

Zee grinned. "Your soil is just richer now, Mackenzie."

The boys all chuckled at that.

"So what are you doing here? Lady troubles?" one of the trio asked him.

"Not me. Bear's got troubles," Mac said, talking about Zee's son, Mac's best friend and owner of the tavern. Mac picked up a damp glass and began drying. "You know he's off chasing after his woman. I'm playing bartender in his place."

"Hope he gets her this time. Your drinks suck." A round of cackles and hoots of laughter followed that remark.

"Whiskey'll cost you double after that," Mac muttered.

"Definitely a woman," the last of the men said.

Mac ignored him. It would take a special kind of woman to get him down, and Mac had yet to meet his match. He glanced at Zee, recalling the older man's happy marriage, one that mirrored the kind his parents had had. Not for the first time, Mac wondered if watching them had given him an idealized perception of what family life should be. Few relationships could live up to the standards he'd seen growing up, and even fewer women respected those same down-to-earth values both families had lived by.

Still, he couldn't deny the fact that hotel life was lonely as hell and beginning to wear thin. Laughter from the corner of the bar drew his attention and he glanced at his watch. Soon enough, the younger crowd would come in and take over. Judging by the increasing noise and the older men's rowdy remarks, it couldn't happen too soon. Mac spent enough time at Bear's bar to know the men were biding their time. Thursday was Ladies' Night, and the eighty-year-old set got a thrill out of watching the younger beauties. They got pretty wild, too, and Mac was grateful he'd be spared wet T-shirt night during this shift.

"If I were you, I'd grab me one of them spa bunnies at that place you own, instead of serving up drinks to old geezers like us."

"You're not me, Earl." Those *spa bunnies* wanted nothing more than a chance to catch some sun and a rich husband. And the ones who already had a husband came to The Resort for a quick fling and whatever else they could get from the guy they earmarked as a sucker.

Not only was Mac tired of watching the routine, he was tired of being the target. Which made his occasional stint as Bear's substitute the perfect escape.

"Another round, Mac," Zee called.

He threw a glance their way. "You aren't halfway through the first." The old men liked their whiskey the way they liked their women. At a distance.

He watched as Zee pushed aside the red-and-white checked curtain to look out the window. The decor could use some updating, Mac thought. Maybe it wouldn't be such a bad thing if Bear finally got his lady after all. At least one of the two neighborhood boys would settle down.

"Looks like we got us a live one." Zee clapped his hands with glee. "Coming up the stairs now."

Mac knew Zee well enough to see past the jokes. The old man had been a father figure to the Mackenzie kids, Mac and his sister, since their own dad had died almost twelve years before. So Mac understood the loneliness that prompted Zee to act a little crazy in his search of fun, and the intelligence and humor that lay behind his penetrating gaze.

But that didn't mean he'd let him harass an unsuspecting customer. "Leave 'em alone, boys."

"You're no fun, Mackenzie," they spoke in chorus, just as the door opened wide and the sorriest sight Mac had ever seen stumbled through.

She was a lady…beneath the layers of desert grime. Black hair tumbled over her shoulders in wild disarray. Her shoes, heels from the looks of them, dangled from her fingertips as she limped inside the bar on long, shapely legs and bare feet.

A quick glance and years of experience told him her skirt was designer, silk and displayed an enticing amount of bare skin. She looked lost and alone in the door frame, with Bear's prize possession, a life-size moose head hanging above her own.

Before he could see any more, the three old men had surrounded her. Mac looked at the ceiling and rolled his eyes, then made his way around the bar. "For God's sake, give the lady some air," he shouted.

The men scattered. And Mac got a firsthand look at the white tank top clinging to her round breasts with exact precision. Thanks to the cold night air, her nipples puckered against the otherwise loose fabric, leaving nothing to the imagination. He had the insane desire to cup his hands over her breasts and warm the lady himself.

He'd gone too damn long without sex if this bedraggled female turned him on. She stared from him to the group in the corner.

"They don't mean any harm." He gestured to the three men ogling her without shame. He knew how they felt.

"Thanks just the same," she said in a husky voice that he'd like to think was sexy by design, but since she'd obviously taken a long hike in the dry desert, she'd probably swallowed more than her share of dust. "My car broke down," she explained.

"Have a seat and I'll get you something cold to

drink," he said. "For your throat. Then you can pour your heart out to a friendly bartender." After which maybe he could find a sweatshirt behind the bar to warm her up and cover her considerable charms. Before he acted on impulse rather than common sense.

She lifted her gaze to his and obviously caught him staring at her chest. A pink flush rose to her cheeks, and she not-so-discreetly crossed her arms in front of her, blocking his view. Her awkward smile disarmed him at the same time he noticed her eyes. The impact sent a jolt of awareness sizzling through him. He'd never seen such an arresting color before, a unique combination of violet and indigo framed by dark lashes and pale skin. Skin marred only by streaks of mascara and what had to be dried tears.

He found himself touched by the sight because this woman was real. Dirty, disheveled and so unlike the women who came to his resort to "rejuvenate" on a regular basis. In his world, a place far removed from the down-to-earth town of his youth, women viewed cosmetic and surgical artifice as the means to keeping their men. Natural beauty like this was too rare.

For once, he looked out and saw someone in need of more than a loaded wallet. "I've got pretty broad shoulders," he said when she remained silent.

"I can see that." Without warning, a smile caught the corners of her mouth and a sparkle settled in those eyes, which now openly appraised him from the top of his black baseball cap to the toes of his running shoes.

Since Bear never required a dress code for employees or patrons of his small establishment, Mac always dressed comfortably. Very comfortably. Mac knew he looked grungy and liked it. Apparently, so did she. He liked that even more.

"I've been walking for a while, and that seat you mentioned does sound awfully good." She did a poor job of fluttering her lashes over makeup-smeared eyes. Damned if he wasn't intrigued...and more than a little turned on. She took a step forward, yelped in what he assumed was pain and collapsed, sagging against him for support.

"I've had women throw themselves at me before, but never like this."

"Maybe because they haven't hiked over a mile in the desert on bare feet," she retorted.

Mac muttered a curse and swung her into his arms.

"Just what do you think you're doing?" She sounded outraged at his chivalry.

"Helping you out, unless you'd like to attempt that step again..." He lowered his hands as if to lower her back down onto the floor.

Soft hands curled around his neck, holding on with an iron grip. She was stronger than she looked.

"Ready to admit you need help?"

She nodded, then settled her body into his, so he felt the soft curve of her breast pressing into his chest and her firm behind nestling against his stomach. If he squirmed, he'd drop her, but ignoring the lingering sensations was damn near impossible.

She tipped her head back and sighed. "My hero."

"Oh, brother." Her hair brushed against his cheek. The scent of peaches clung to her skin despite her trek through the desert. His effort to block out the surge of sexual awareness that shot through him failed dismally.

Mac deposited her in the nearest chair, then lifted her foot for inspection. He ran a finger along the cut and bruised arch. Her startled gaze met his.

"I have antiseptic and gauze upstairs," he said in a husky voice. Or at least, he knew Bear did. His friend had broken up many late-night brawls, and Mac had often hung around to help clean the place, and his pal, up afterward.

"Upstairs?" she squeaked. Then she quickly cleared her throat and started over. "Upstairs where? A room? An apartment? What?" Her curiosity seemed to overtake her initial doubts and she peppered him with questions, growing more confident with each.

"An apartment," he said, amused.

"With a shower?"

He raised an eyebrow. "Shower and tub, why?"

"Curiosity. And you live there?" she asked, now wide-eyed.

"Yeah." For the week, or as long as it took Bear to win his lady back. For reasons he didn't want to inspect too closely, Mac decided against telling her that he was only helping out. It had been a long time since he'd been known and liked as plain Mac, separate and apart from Ryan Mackenzie, owner of The Resort.

He'd be the first to admit his own mistakes contributed to the problem. Wealth had come to the Mackenzies when Mac had been too brash and arrogant to understand how people, namely women, would react. A single, rich resort owner was a prime catch, and he'd stupidly made himself a target for gold diggers and fortune hunters alike.

Taking care of his mother and younger sister had forced him to realize his mistakes and grow up fast. The females in his family had relied on him for financial security and emotional backing. He couldn't afford to let them down, and after his initial lapse in judgment, he hadn't. Mac had trained himself to be wary, which was why he remained silent now.

This woman's vulnerability appealed to him, and he wanted a fresh read, a chance to be liked as an ordinary guy with no preconceived notions getting in the way.

He glanced over. She sat fiddling with the top layer of her skirt. "Do you live alone?" she asked, this time without meeting his gaze.

"Completely."

"Oh. Oh. Good." A blush made its way through the dirt and makeup that stained her cheeks.

From embarrassed to brazen and back again, he thought. "Good?"

"For my feet." She forced herself to stand on her own. "And my dignity. Do you think I could wash up?" she asked.

He nodded. "While you're at it, I'll send a tow for the car and I'll have one of the boys pick up your suitcases."

"The boys?"

"They surrounded you when you first came in. Now they're eyeballing you from across the room."

She grinned. "Oh, those boys. They drive?"

"Not legally."

Her laughter filled the room and a few other places inside him he'd thought were frozen for good. "About those suitcases," she said. "How do you know I have any?"

"Sweetheart…" His gaze trailed over her shapely body and white skin. "Everything about you screams tourist."

He reached out to help her walk, but she shook her head.

"I can do this."

"Okay, but I'm right behind you if you need any help. Up those stairs." He pointed to the darkened hallway in the corner, and she headed off in that direction, unsteady on her feet. "One of you boys watch the bar," he called to the group of regulars that Bear trusted as much as he did his best friend.

Mac stared at her retreating back, watched as she climbed the stairs, leaving him on the step below. Her silken skirt ended midthigh, which wasn't a problem when they were on the same level. But he hadn't anticipated the view once she hit the middle of the stairs. Nor had he realized how sexy and feminine her undergarments would be. As the short skirt flounced behind her, a hint of lace teased and tormented his already-active libido. Heat rolled over him in a huge wave. He broke into a sweat.

And to think, he'd almost refused to help Bear because he had a number of huge conventions arriving throughout the week. He was glad he'd delegated to his staff, entrusting the numerous doctors, lawyers and financiers to his employees. He wouldn't have missed this for anything.

As he followed his sexy, straggly visitor upstairs, he realized he'd seen more of her than he'd seen of any other woman in a long while. And he didn't even know her name.

SHE'D FOUND HER MAN. Too bad she had no idea what to do with him. Samantha closed the bathroom door behind her and stripped off her skirt, shaking the residual dust into the tub. Who'd have guessed the first man she laid eyes on, the first man under eighty, she amended, would be the one?

Her questions hadn't exactly been subtle, but with those dark, deep-set eyes staring into hers, and that mustache lifting over a sensual grin, she'd barely been able to pull herself together enough to think clearly.

She pictured him waiting on the other side of the door, and her pulse pounded in a combination of anticipation and apprehension. There was no question the dark-haired, gorgeous stranger suited her perfectly. A bartender in an off-the-beaten-path tavern, he was a man she could thoroughly enjoy and then never see again. As long as she could work up the nerve.

Samantha located the towels he said would be on a shelf over the toilet, and hung one over a hook on the wall. She glanced around the room. Small but with all the proper amenities and stark in a masculine sort of way. No frills. Just a toothbrush and a bottle of aftershave lay on top of the vanity. She picked up the black bottle and brought the nozzle near her nose. One illicit sniff of musk and she was no longer alone. *His* scent surrounded her. *He* surrounded her.

She'd never been with a man wearing a mustache and wondered what kind of stimulation it would add to an intense sexual experience? She shut her eyes. Her senses soared and her imagination took over. Soft lips, warm breath and an erotic rush of sensation playing over her already-sensitized skin. Firm yet gentle lips nibbling their way up her legs, the rasp of whiskers along her thigh. She cupped her breasts and felt as if his hands had settled over the tight fabric, as if his fingers plucked and pulled, bringing her nipples to life.

She opened her eyes to find herself standing alone in the unfamiliar bathroom, thoroughly aroused and completely appalled. She had *never* done anything like this before, had never even *felt* anything like this before. Without meeting her gaze in the mirror, she removed her hands from her chest and focused her attention on turning on the shower instead.

Her hands trembled, hindering the process. How could she want one man so badly? A man she barely knew. She didn't know the answer to that question any more than she knew how she'd find the nerve to go through with this seduction. Coming up with her plan from the safety of her apartment had been easy. Contemplating her bleak future had carried her resolve through the long plane ride out here. But now, faced with a sexy, masculine stranger in the flesh…

Samantha trembled. All she had left was this

week. She hadn't planned her life this way, nor would this be the choice she'd make if her father's future weren't at stake. *But it was*. And if her life came down to this one week, she'd better make the most of it. Her chance waited just outside the door.

If she wanted to find a way into his arms, she'd best start by cleaning herself up. But first, she needed to get a drink to soothe her parched throat, she thought, reaching for a nearby glass and filling it with water. That decided, she felt more confident. In a few hours, if she was lucky, she'd discover...how to scare the poor man half to death. Samantha caught a glimpse of her face in the mirror and gasped, dropping the glass into the sink. With her dirt-streaked cheeks, tearstains and tangled mass of hair, how could she have considered seducing him? Whatever made her think he'd be interested?

Without warning, the door burst open and she had company. "What the hell was that?"

Her grab for the towel came too late because her fantasy lover stood in the door frame staring at her practically naked body. Okay, he'd seen her shirt before, but the sexy underwear, her one concession to femininity beneath the tailored suits she wore to work, left her midriff completely exposed. She glanced down. The small triangular scrap of material between her legs showed more than she wanted him to see at the present time.

"Well?"

She didn't answer. She couldn't. Not if her life depended on it. She was more concerned with covering herself. She tried to remove the towel from the hook on the wall, but the shaking of her hands hindered the attempt.

She turned to gain better leverage and heard his sharp intake of breath.

"Those things ought to be outlawed."

Her hands went to her behind, covered only by flimsy lace with scalloped edging, and at that moment, Samantha discovered she wasn't as brave as she'd planned to be. She was mortified.

How could she even think she could seduce a man? Nothing showed like inexperience, and though she'd had relationships before, she'd never tackled a one-night stand. After the impression she'd made, she wouldn't be doing so tonight.

She'd blown her chance and devastated her ego. Not bad for a night's work.

He brushed past her. A powerful dose of his masculine scent overwhelmed her like an aphrodisiac. As if she needed more than just a look to arouse her beyond belief.

He yanked the towel off the hook, making the maneuver look easy. "Cover yourself," he growled.

Startled by his tone, she turned to look at him. His eyes had darkened, the smoky gray transformed into deep charcoal. Color highlighted his cheekbones and those firm-looking lips were pulled into a tight line.

"Now." He shook the towel before her eyes. "Or I won't be responsible for my actions."

"Yes, sir." Her gaze slipped to his waist and the telltale bulge in his tight jeans. Pure female pleasure stirred inside her. Her technique might need work, but she hadn't botched things after all. Her doubts scattered, along with her short bout of self-pity. This man wanted her, and she refused to question her good fortune.

Taking her time, she accepted the towel, wrapping the soft terry around her body until she could tuck the free end between her breasts. "Done," she said, with what she hoped was a flirtatious smile.

A hoarse groan escaped her companion. "Time's up," he muttered.

Samantha swallowed hard. "It is?" To her chagrin, her voice trembled when she spoke. "You mean, now?"

She'd given him the location of her car and the keys, and she'd hoped to have clean clothes in which to seduce him. Her plans hadn't included his take-charge personality. The differences between fantasy and reality came back to haunt her again. She wasn't ready.

She'd have preferred a little get-to-know-you time first. She'd have liked a shower. Obviously, he had no need for such prerequisites, and nervousness once again replaced her prior certainty.

Yet when he held out his hand, she placed hers inside the large, warm palm. Touching him provided a sensual pleasure she couldn't have imagined. If she allowed herself to think about what was to come, she'd pass out on the tile floor. His long fingers wrapped around her smaller hand. Fingers she had no doubt could bring great pleasure.

"Well?" he asked.

"Well, what?" He couldn't possibly expect her to make the first move. She licked her lips, uncomfortably aware of the small bathroom space and his overpowering presence.

"Can we get on with this before the room becomes a sauna?"

Apparently the man wasn't into preliminaries. Samantha hoped he liked to bask in the afterglow, because the way things were going, this wasn't going to be the slow, sensual experience she'd envisioned.

"I don't think…"

"Oh, for God's sake. You don't want to go first, I will. My name's Mac," he said, shaking her hand with a determined grip. "What's yours?"

CHAPTER TWO

MAC STOOD IN THE DOOR frame of the small bath-room, unable to believe he'd burst in without warn-ing. When he'd heard the shatter of glass, he figured she'd come face-to-face with a rodent of some kind. Instead, she stood half dressed, staring at him as if he'd invaded her privacy. Which, considering the room she was in and her state of undress, he had.

"My...name?" She blinked, obviously startled.

"Yeah. I've seen pretty much everything, sweet-heart." And he knew what she looked like when she was cold. His gaze inadvertently went to her chest, now covered by layers of terry cloth. "I doubt tell-ing me your name would be considered a breach of etiquette."

She blushed scarlet. "Sam..." She paused in thought. "Just Sam."

She hadn't removed her hand from his, and he let his thumb drift over her skin. She didn't seem to mind, or she was too flustered to notice. Either way, he liked the way her palm fit into his.

"Sam." He played with the name, tossing it around in his mind, savoring it on his lips. Then he thought of the rounded breasts and the darkened nipples visible beneath the white top. His imagination conjured two perfectly shaped, creamy white cheeks. A masculine name didn't suit her and he shook his head. "Doesn't work for me. Short for Samantha?" he guessed.

She exhaled loudly. "Yes. But that doesn't work for me."

He smiled, enjoying this woman, if not yet understanding her. "Mind if I ask why not?"

"I'm on vacation, and I'd like to forget the people who call me that…at least for this week."

A runaway like himself. He understood the need to escape from life, work and the people who occupied those other worlds. Family gave Mac the best alternative, but they weren't close enough to offer a quick reprieve. Courtesy of her husband's job, his sister's family lived a couple of hours away, and with the birth of his first nephew, Mac's mother had moved out of the hotel to be closer to Kate. With his only family miles away—including a new baby he didn't see nearly often enough—Mac understood his recent restlessness. In fact, it was almost as if he was itching to settle down himself.

Short of that, Bear's place was his best and closest means of escape. He glanced at the woman whose hand he still held, wondering how far she'd run. And from what. "And after the week's up?" he asked.

She shrugged. "I go back to my life."

"To being Samantha."

"That's right." She pulled her hand back and hugged her arms around the fluffy towel. "I haven't had a vacation in years. So I thought I'd take a little time for myself before I go to a conference next weekend."

"Name someone who isn't in town for a conference. Arizona has become the convention capital Florida used to be." Which was why he was so successful.

His father had purchased desert land dirt cheap in the mid-1950s. After the older man's death, Mac had sold a small portion for much more than he'd ever imagined, and expanded the small bed-and-breakfast inn that had been his family's livelihood. By catering to the vacationer and the conference-goer, The Resort had become a gold mine. And the once-middle-income Mackenzies, Mac, his mother and sister, had become millionaires.

A fact he had no intention of revealing to Samantha until he got to know her better. "Okay, *Sam*." She nodded her approval. "Now that we have that behind us, we can move on." On impulse, he raised her hand to his mouth and pressed a kiss on her wrist. Her pulse fluttered wildly beneath his lips.

She jerked her hand free. "No, we can't. I just met you and I'm not about to hop into your bed." She didn't speak with much conviction, nor did she seem to realize the leap she'd made.

"That's good, because I don't remember inviting you," he said with a hearty laugh. "But trust me. When I do…you'll know it."

"Oh…" She stared at him, wide-eyed and embarrassed.

Mac had never seen such mixed signals. Earlier, she'd appraised his body as if it were meat in the deli case. She wore sexy underwear he'd never seen anywhere but in a catalog, sensual clothing that invited seduction, yet she was holding on to that towel with a death grip. He deliberately tuned out the memory of what she looked like without it. For now.

The innocent or the seductress. Which woman was his Samantha? He couldn't think of her as *Sam* any more than he should be thinking of her as his. But he liked the contradictions in her character and wanted her to stick around.

After suffering the attentions of too many fortune-hunting women, he was intrigued by her honest responses. But before he seduced her he had to be sure.

"I was trying to suggest you take a shower." He backed off, walking toward the door.

"Mac, wait."

He turned.

"I'm sorry. I'm new at this…I guess you can tell, what with me jumping to conclusions and rambling and…"

He stepped back inside the small room, effectively silencing her with his presence. Walking toward her he stood close enough to temptation to make himself sweat…without the aid of the steam-filled bathroom. Unable to help himself, he reached forward and took a lock of ebony hair, wrapping the satin strands around his finger as he spoke.

The pulse at the base of her throat worked overtime. "New at what?" he asked.

"This. Whatever's happening between us." She gestured to them both.

"Is there something between us?" After her vehement rejection, he needed to know what she wanted before pursuing anything further.

Her violet gaze met his. Honesty and sincerity shimmered in their depths. "You know there is."

He admired the strength it took for her to admit there was something brewing, even though the pull between them was too strong to ignore.

"And what are we going to do about it?" He unraveled her hair from his finger and ran the fine ends over the skin beneath her jaw. "Sam?" He breathed her name, suddenly finding it important to respect this woman's wishes.

A tremor shook her body and she sighed softly. "I don't know." She leaned forward, until they were separated by a fraction of air.

Body language was telling and Mac had his answer. He wanted to close the distance between them. He needed to taste her lips and learn her secrets, and he had a hunch this intriguing woman had many. But her answer wasn't good enough.

He looked into her soft eyes. She wanted him, but there were things she needed more. Like a shower and some time to herself.

"You think about it…and let me know." He straightened and dropped her hair, letting his fingers graze her shoulder as he did. "The rental place is sending out a replacement car. In the meantime, I'll leave your suitcases in the next room. Come on downstairs once you're cleaned up."

She smiled. "Thanks. You're a nice guy, Mac."

He groaned. He wasn't nice, he was horny. Which made him wonder what it was about this woman that had him acting so noble. He had no doubt that with some soft words and coaxing hands, he could have been inside her body.

Instead he was headed downstairs to a bar full of customers, a bunch of nosy old men and one major problem, he discovered when he hit the bottom step.

"What do you mean, Theresa's waiting to talk to me?" Mac looked over Zee's shoulder to where his one-

and-only cocktail waitress sat nervously shredding a paper napkin to bits. "Shouldn't she be working?"

"She's served a few glasses while you were upstairs. Broke a few, too," Zee muttered.

"Why the slippery fingers?"

"She didn't like Hardy's hand on her rump." The old man's cackle filled his ears, but his expression quickly sobered. "Her Mama broke her hip coming out of the tub and her mind's not on work."

Mac muttered a curse, knowing he couldn't keep Theresa here when she was needed at home. Even if this was one of the busiest nights. "I'll talk to her. Anything else I should know?"

"Hardy's behind the bar watering down the drinks. Earl's downing more than he's serving, and the sexy lady's luggage is in the corner," Zee informed him.

"And what are you doing?"

"Checking IDs at the door. Less than a C-cup means no entry." The old man grinned.

"Come on, Zee. You know we can't discriminate. On Ladies' Night, it's illegal. If they even have a cup size, let 'em in free."

His chuckle pleased Mac. Better than seeing the old guy moping and depressed, Mac thought. He loved the man who'd treated him as well as he treated his own son.

"Want me to take the lady her bags?"

"No, thanks, I can handle it." Mac didn't trust
Zee not to sneak a peek, so he brought Samantha's
luggage upstairs on his own. Not that he wasn't
tempted to catch a glimpse himself, but the large
crowd and an obligation to his friend had him running down the back stairs to work. If Samantha was
a typical woman when it came to getting ready, he
wouldn't be seeing her for a while.

Since he definitely needed some time to get his
libido under control, he didn't mind. He'd given the
lady time to decide. It didn't matter that his body pro-
tested with throbbing intensity. *Nice guys* lived uncomfortably by their word…and they didn't get
lucky, either. Resettling his cap on his head, Mac
rounded the corner of the bar and got to work.

Not fifteen minutes later, the woman who'd
caused his aroused state walked back into the bar. He
should have known. There was nothing typical about
his Samantha.

SHE GRABBED THE FIRST cushioned bar stool she
could find, not an easy task on Ladies' Night, and
propped her arms on the bar. Beneath her elbows,
pennies, Abe Lincoln-side up, stared at her from
under the scratched glass. Sam—she decided the
name fit and she intended to keep it—was enchanted
by the timeworn ambience of the bar.

Used to frequenting places like Lincoln Center

and upscale restaurants in New York, she appreciated the chance to kick back and relax in a comfortable setting. *Relaxing* was a relative term, since Mac stood not a few feet away at the end of the bar, engrossed in conversation with a young woman. Judging by the white apron tied around her waist, the woman was his cocktail waitress and she didn't look happy.

Although Sam couldn't hear their conversation, it was obviously serious. Mac shook his head, then made his way to the cash register and handed money to the woman, who tried to push the cash back into his hands. Mac refused. The young woman then threw her arms around his neck, hugging him tight.

Whatever had transpired between them was obviously business, and yet the twisting in Sam's stomach when the other woman touched Mac couldn't be ignored. Feeling like an outsider, not to mention a jealous female—and not liking either—Sam shrugged and turned her attention away. Seconds later, Mac returned to the center of the bar.

He immediately began hustling between customers, serving liquor to smiling females. Sam could drink in his quick, sure movements all night. He was a study in masculine grace, if there was such a thing, easily grabbing glasses and tipping bottles as if he'd been doing this all his life. For all she knew, he had been.

Not for the first time, she realized she knew noth-

ing about this man, except he set her body on fire
with a sizzling look and, on some level, she trusted
him. She'd be a fool to sleep with him otherwise.

She knew Mac could provide passion. His touch
set off heated sparks and his voice shook her soul. If
she wanted fun, excitement and hot nights in bed,
she'd fallen into the right bar. *Think about it...and
let me know.* Yearning mixed with trepidation. All she
had to do was push her fears aside long enough to
make the first move. The thought of Tom and a lifetime of single beds or separate rooms if she could
manage it, clinched her decision.

"Hey, honey. Can I buy you a drink?"

She recognized one of the old men who'd cor-
nered her when she first came in. "Sure."

"Hey, Mac," the old guy yelled across the crowded
bar. "Two shots of tequila...and don't forget the
lemon."

Mac turned their way long enough to raise an eyebrow at the request before finishing off other orders
and making his way toward them. A nervous knot
settled in the pit of her stomach. Her throat went dry,
and Sam knew what she wanted. That was the easy
part.

Letting him know would be harder.

He paused directly in front of her, bracing his
hands on the old wood. Even the dark hair on his
arms intrigued her, making her wonder what the tex-

ture would feel like if she ran her hands along his bare chest. "Tequila?"

She shrugged nonchalantly, though she felt anything but. "That's what the man said."

"That's Zee to you, honey. And none of that watered-down crap Bear usually gives us," he told Mac.

Mac glanced at her. "You sure about that?"

"Why not?"

"Ever drink tequila before?"

She shook her head.

"That's why." But he began working on their order, turning over two shot glasses and filling them with amber-colored liquid.

"Who's Bear?" Sam asked.

"The guy who owns this joint," Zee said.

"Your employer?"

"He owns the place and I'm working it. You tell me." Mac set the glasses down in front of them, along with a saltshaker and a bowl of lemons. He slid the rest of the bottle over to Zee. "Go easy," he said, and turned to the people next to her.

The bar crowd had more than quadrupled since she'd arrived, and Mac worked the room alone without a moment's break. "He looks overworked."

Zee nodded. "And underpaid."

"I heard that." Mac shot the old man a quelling look.

She tipped her head to the side. "Hard work's nothing to be ashamed of."

"He gave his cocktail waitress the night off," Zee explained.

"I thought I just saw her here," Sam said.

"You did. But Mac here thought she'd be better off baby-sitting her sick mama than catering to us old men. Even paid her the night's wages...though she won't make any tips."

And that explained the transaction she'd witnessed earlier along with the woman's *hug of gratitude*. Sam felt like a jerk.

She blinked and looked at Mac, who'd gone back to serving other customers.

"That was nice of him," she murmured. She'd not only stumbled onto a sexy man, but he played Sir Galahad, to boot. Warmth spread through her as she acknowledged that this man had character as well as good looks.

"Boy's got a heart of gold. Always has. 'Course, it doesn't make up for his sour disposition."

Mac paused in front of them. "You bring out the best in me, old man," he chuckled wryly. The light in his eyes and the laugh lines bracketing his mouth sent tremors of awareness shooting toward strategic body parts, making her sizzle and burn. She'd never felt anything like it before. Samantha rubbed her hands up and down her bare arms.

Zee ignored him and glanced at the still-full glasses. "You gonna sit there all night or you gonna give me a run for my money? Watch and learn, honey."

Sam had seen this maneuver in college, but she'd never witnessed an eighty-year-old man make the attempt. Zee performed admirably. "You sure he's up to this?" she asked Mac as Zee wiped his mouth on his sleeve.

"Apparently more than you."

She took that as a challenge. Copying the old man, she licked her hand, poured the salt onto her skin, licked, downed the contents of the shot glass and reached for the lemon.

"Not bad for a first-timer," Zee congratulated, refilling the glasses.

Sam's gaze met Mac's the moment the sour fruit reached her lips...because she'd just gulped a mouthful of straight water mixed with a healthy dose of food coloring. And he knew it. He winked, telling her to play along.

In that instant, Sam got another glimpse into her knight in shining armor's character. He humored old men and looked out for damsels in distress. Considering her current predicament, Sam realized she fit that label, too.

Mac, whatever-his-last-name-was, was a sexy, hard-working, sexy, *decent,* sexy guy. The perfect man for her purposes. Sam liked what she saw and liked what she'd learned. She couldn't have found a better man than Mac.

But first he had a bar to run, and from the look of things, he needed help.

OUT OF BEER. The ladies in The Hungry Bear never ceased to amaze him. The Resort stocked premium vodka, while Bear loaded up on dark beer. Same state, different breed of women, Mac thought as he headed for the back room to refill his supply.

He'd moved one box to get to the keg when a fragrant scent alerted him that he had company. He raised his head, but without looking over his shoulder, he knew. Samantha.

"What are you doing here?" he asked, without turning around. She was a distraction he couldn't enjoy right now. Later, when he locked up for the night, maybe. If she was willing. But not now.

"A couple just walked in and they wanted a beer. The tap was empty and I didn't see any bottles behind the bar, so I…"

"You were tending bar?"

"There wasn't anyone else to do it." She squared her shoulders defensively.

"I told Zee to keep an eye on things."

"Zee thinks he's drunk."

That comment broke the tension, and they shared

a good laugh. "You look out for him," she said. Approval and something more gleamed in her eyes, making him uncomfortable beneath her knowing stare.

"Someone has to...he's Bear's father. The old guy lost his wife a few years back and he's always looking for a little attention. It was nice of you to give it to him, by the way." Not many people would give a lonely old man the time of day. Bear's customers put up with the old coot for Bear's sake and because like Mac, they'd known Zee and his friends forever. Samantha had done it for a stranger.

"How long had they been married?" she asked.

"Over fifty years."

"Wow, that's a long time." A shudder shook her slight frame.

"Not for them. They really loved each other." Mac wondered when he'd become the spokesperson for marriage. Not that he'd mind settling down one day; in fact, he'd like nothing more. He just never believed he'd find a woman sincere and honest enough to make the risk worthwhile. He glanced at Samantha. Until now?

Mac wanted the chance to find out.

"At least those years were filled with love," she said.

He met her gaze. "Can't see tying yourself to someone for any other reason. Might as well wrap a noose around your neck otherwise."

She cleared her throat. "Would you mind changing the subject?"

"Why? Marriage makes you uncomfortable?" he asked lightly. If he had his way, he'd have plenty of time later to pry her secrets out of her. She obviously had many. "Don't tell Zee or he'll be giving you an earful about tradition, respect and good old-fashioned love." The older man's distinctive cackle filtered into the room.

She smiled, the wide grin knocking him senseless. There was no way he'd survive until closing with her hanging around, dodging his every move.

"He's harmless...and sweet." She shut the door behind her and walked inside, moving closer until he caught a whiff of the tangy soap she'd used during her shower. Though he missed the hint of peaches clinging to her skin, this scent worked on him, too.

She drew a deep breath. "Kind of like you," she murmured, a nervous tremor touching her voice.

He lifted her chin with his finger. "Sweetheart, I'm the furthest thing from sweet you'll find in these parts." Cold, withdrawn, disinterested. Those were the nicer adjectives some of the women at The Resort used to describe the blunt manner in which he'd turned down their advances. But he'd learned the hard way, letting them down gently never worked.

"Why don't you let me be the judge of that." She braced her hands on his shoulders and pushed him back until he hit the wall. Then with another tremulous breath, she leaned her body against his.

And then she kissed him. Hard and fast, as if she didn't want to give herself a chance to change her mind. Which was fine with him. She'd made the first move, and Mac intended to make sure she didn't regret it. Because with her soft mouth devouring his and her hands now pulling at his shirt and trailing up his chest, he definitely wanted more.

She didn't give him a chance. Those fingers curled into fists and she shoved backward, separating them before he could act on impulse and take what he wanted. What she'd seemed to offer just seconds before.

Wide eyes, darkened by passion and a hint of insecurity, met his. "I don't know what I was thinking, grabbing you like that."

Her uncertainty touched him. "I don't know what you were thinking, either, but did you hear me complaining?"

A slight smile took hold of her lips. "You mean you liked it?" she asked.

Reaching out, he grasped her forearm, gently pressing his fingers into her flesh. "You mean you couldn't tell? My technique must be rusty." He let his thumb run circles over her skin.

He took one step toward her, and when she didn't back away, he locked them together once again. She tipped her head backward to meet his gaze.

"You can trust me, sweetheart."

"I know." Her wide smile reassured him, and he kissed her without holding back. She responded. Her tongue filled his mouth, while her soft sighs and little moans drove him mad. Apparently she'd needed reassurance, and having gotten it, she relaxed in his arms.

Her flimsy shirt already hung off one bare shoulder. Although not blatantly sexy, this soft, frilly thing aroused him beyond belief. Acting on impulse, he grabbed both the tank top strap along with the ruffled edge of the shirt and pulled both down far enough to let him taste one of her darkened nipples. Her moan of delight was unrestrained as she arched her back in wanton response, giving him complete access.

Mac had never embarrassed himself in front of a woman, but he damn near did so now. Another few seconds and he wouldn't give a damn that a bar full of people waited outside that door. He'd scatter their clothes on the floor and bury himself inside her willing warmth. He needed to stop but wasn't ready to let her go.

He had no choice. Her admitted hesitancy prevented him from going further. With more difficulty than he would have imagined, he raised his head. "Still think I'm harmless?" he asked, his breathing not at all steady.

"No, but you do taste sweet." An embarrassed smile played over her lips. "I wasn't sure how to approach you…but I'm glad I did."

He'd been right. For all her attempts at seduction, she was very new at this kind of game. Which made him wonder what other secrets she kept. She'd already admitted to being a temporary runaway. And given the inexperience he sensed and the innocence she projected, he had to wonder why the urgency to come on to him at all? Every unanswered question made her all the more fascinating.

He met her gaze. Her violet eyes were still glazed with a combination of passion and disbelief. Mac understood. He'd never have believed they'd make such an explosive combination, either. He hadn't thought this bundle of contradictions had it in her. He'd sensed her hesitancy and figured she'd bail out. Instead, she'd come to him. To Mac, the bartender.

If his instincts were on, this hot, blazing desire that flared between them was just as new to her as it was to… No. No. He shook his head. Desire wasn't new to him. He'd wanted before. He'd just never come so close so fast.

He had the unnerving sense that one night with Samantha wouldn't be enough to douse this high-charged inferno that blazed out of control. Worse, he wasn't sure he wanted it to be. But until he understood what she was running from and why, he couldn't take advantage…no matter how badly he wanted to.

With deliberate slowness, he picked her up and lowered her to the ground, making sure their bodies touched the entire time. Making sure she felt the hard ridge of his arousal. Her sharp inhale told him she had.

She'd pulled her still-damp hair into a braid that touched her shoulder. He toyed with the end. "It's wet."

"I didn't want to take time to dry it."

He played with her hair, running the strands down her cheek and along her neck, then following the path with his tongue. He looked up and met her wide-eyed gaze. "Where are you planning on staying?" he asked.

She cleared her throat. "Wherever I'm welcome."

She was welcome here. The thought shocked him, but he realized he meant it. Keeping her around would give him time to get to know this woman, something he wanted, nearly as much as he desired her.

He bent his head. "The bed upstairs is a double," he whispered in her ear.

Mac told himself it made sense. She needed a place to stay. He needed to keep her around. As difficult as it would be, he could keep a respectable physical distance between them. She might think she wanted more, but her eyes mirrored her soul, and she was still unsure. Not of the sexual chemistry, because they'd steamed up this stockroom in no time at all, of something deeper. Emotionally, she wasn't ready for more.

When the stakes were high, and the prize worth winning, Mac had an abundance of patience. "Well?" he asked her.

"I..." He bit on her earlobe and her shudder went straight through him. "I check in next Thursday morning," she managed to say. "My conference begins at eight on Friday."

Loud banging on the door interrupted them before things got out of control. "I may be old, but my memory's fine. It doesn't take that long," Zee yelled. "You got thirsty people out here."

Her face flushed scarlet, and Mac cupped her cheeks in his palms. "He's wrong."

"He is?" Her voice was filled with breathless anticipation.

Mac nodded. "It'll take the whole week. I'll make sure of it," he said in a voice he barely recognized.

Then he turned and walked out, leaving her to pull herself together while he hoped nobody else noticed how long he'd been gone. Or that he'd forgotten the beer. Or that he wanted Samantha so badly he could hardly walk. This woman, her honesty and vulnerability, made him believe in a future for the first time in years. Combine that with a sexual chemistry fierce enough to set his soul on fire, and Mac knew exactly why he'd invited her to stay for the duration.

Never before had a bartending favor held so much promise. As Mac got back to work, he wondered if anyone would notice if he skipped last call.

CHAPTER THREE

SAM WIPED DOWN the table and pocketed the tip left beneath the glass. As quickly as she'd taken over Theresa's job, she'd fallen into a steady rhythm. She wasn't half bad at cocktail waitressing. The overall pace here was slower than back home, which made for an easier transition. She enjoyed the customers, and they seemed to like talking with her. An easterner provided them with a source of amusement for the evening, and their slight accents intrigued her.

"Hey, honey. Another one in the corner."

Sam rolled her eyes. She had no idea where Zee got his endless supply of energy. Hers was dwindling fast. She ducked behind the bar in search of Mac's secret supply of Zee's liquor.

"You holding up okay?"

Her heart tripped in reaction to the husky voice. Good thing her feet didn't do the same or she'd lose her night's take paying for the damage. She turned toward Mac. "I'm fine."

"You had a rough walk over here." His gaze lingered on her canvas sneakers. His caring amazed her. The man needed a cocktail waitress or he'd have had to close down earlier, yet he'd sent Theresa home, and now here he was concerned about a few cuts and bruises on her feet—the feet of a woman he'd just met.

He had a soft spot beneath the rougher exterior. Sam liked that about him. Too much, considering.

"Tell the boys this is last call," he said.

She nearly kissed him in relief, but with a bar full of people, and their last session still fresh in her mind, she pushed the idea aside. As she went to serve her last drinks and clean up the increasingly empty tables, her nerves prickled with the awareness of being watched. The sensation only heightened as the night wore on, until just thinking about Mac sent her senses into heated overload.

Finally, she shut the door behind the last paying customer of the night. Without turning, she heard the sound of the stools being swung on top of the bar. Mac preparing to clean the floors, she assumed. She couldn't face him. Not with her emotions so fragile after the way she'd attacked him in the storage room earlier.

"And especially not after agreeing to spend the week in his bed," she muttered aloud.

The bar had been so busy, that except for his intense gaze and the times she needed to request orders, she'd managed to avoid anything personal between them for the rest of the night. Of course if she stayed here, she'd have to look him in the eye sooner or later.

Who was she kidding? If she stayed here, she'd be looking at a lot more than dark eyes framed by incredibly long lashes. She'd be looking at Mac. All of him.

Well, she'd wanted hot. She'd wanted to experience excitement and passion. He'd given her firsthand proof he could provide all three. The memory invited a rhythmic pounding and accompanying dampness between her legs. She refused to walk away now, even though guilt threatened her plans. Her conscience had picked an awful time to kick in.

She might not love Tom, and he might have bribed her into this engagement, but Samantha took commitment seriously. Throwing herself at one man while engaged to another bothered her more than she cared to admit. But not enough to change her mind. And she sensed *that* decision had more to do with Mac than the need for a one-week fling. She wanted this time with *this* man.

Tom would never know, and except for his ego, she wondered if he'd even care. Each of them would provide a function in the other's life. She would be a trophy to hang on his arm, he would give her the cash to bail out her father. She was the only one not personally gaining from the deal.

"Except for the fact that it led me to you," she murmured. Her gaze darted toward Mac's broad back. Muscles in his upper arms and neck flexed as he worked. Strong and self-confident as he was, she doubted he'd appreciate knowing that technically she belonged to another man.

She ran her thumb over her temporarily bare ring finger. She didn't like thinking of herself in terms of ownership, but she knew how men viewed the world. A man like Mac might get picky over little details—like her upcoming wedding. Since she'd never see him again afterward, there was no reason to risk losing this once-in-a-lifetime chance.

"Sammy Jo, come do one more shot before I let Hardy drive me home." She rolled her eyes. She never should have told Zee he could call her by that ridiculous name.

"Sammy Jo?"

"Samantha Josephine," Zee said. "You want to get to know a lady, you have to ask the right questions."

"Sammy Jo." Mac leaned on the handle of a large mop as he studied her. His heated gaze swept over her body, lingering on places he had no business observing in public. Places he'd seen earlier that evening. She had the definite impression he was remembering much more than what was currently before his eyes. "Sammy Jo," he said again, this time in a much more seductive, huskier voice. "Now, *that* works for me."

Her name on his lips worked for her, too, in any form. Forcing herself to break eye contact, she turned to her drinking buddy. "I'm sorry, Zee, but I'm done for the night." She couldn't swallow another glass of water without her bladder exploding. As much as she liked the old guy and enjoyed his company, she'd humored him enough for one evening.

With a forced smile, she looked at Zee and hiccuped. Loud.

Mac chuckled. Zee grinned. "Told you I could drink her under the table. 'Night, all. Catch you tomorrow." He walked out of the bar, his designated driver hot on his heels.

Mac closed the door behind him and turned the dead bolt shut. Talk about defining moments, Sam thought. From now on, she'd associate the sound of a lock clicking into place with this man and this night.

"Alone at last." He adjusted the brim of his baseball cap and grinned. Then he crooked a finger in her direction. "Come here…Sammy Jo."

His dark eyes glittered with unchecked desire. Her heart threatened to explode in her chest, but she walked toward him, transfixed by the heat in his gaze and the way he made her body ache with one searing look.

Three steps, maybe four, and she reached him. Without prelude, he cupped his hands over her cheeks and kissed her. His tongue worked its way into her already-open mouth and sought hers. Sam expected a hard, demanding kiss, much like the ones they'd shared earlier. She could have handled one of those.

But the tender way he kissed her, learning the deep recesses of her mouth and then nibbling on her lower lip until she nearly cried at the unexpected sweetness of the assault—well, that she couldn't handle at all. When he lifted his head, his gaze caught and held hers.

She couldn't catch her breath, so she didn't try. As for the lump in her throat, she swallowed and attempted to talk over it. "What was that for?" she asked.

"You looked uncertain and I wanted to make sure you remembered why."

She didn't have to ask "Why what?" Why she'd plastered her body to his earlier. Why she'd agreed to stay with him. Why she shouldn't change her mind. He had no way of knowing she already knew. *He* was the answer to all those questions. His incredible masculinity and the chemistry she could generate only with him. She'd come west on a mission of sorts, but even in her wildest, most erotic dreams, she'd never imagined Mac.

He grasped her by the waist and settled her on one of the few stools still standing on the floor. Thanks to her loose, flowing top, his hands cupped bare skin, and the touch made her long for more. Instead his hands went to her feet, and he unlaced and pulled off her sneaker. He massaged her aching arch through her white sock.

She leaned back against the bar and sighed with delight. "Wow, that feels good."

He groaned. "I could think of lots of things that would feel better, but something tells me you need this more."

"You know a lot about someone you just met." She was still thinking about the reassuring kiss, not her sore feet.

"You're easy to read."

She forced her heavy eyelids open. "I'm not sure I like the sound of that." Because he wasn't, which made this a very one-sided relationship. Whoa. Not a relationship. A one-night stand or, if things worked out, one week. But not a relationship, which implied long-term commitment. She was already embroiled in one of those.

Sam didn't like the way her thoughts were going, and she tried to concentrate on her feet instead, which wasn't difficult, since he'd pulled off her other shoe and settled in to work. His hands massaged and coaxed along her arch and up her calves.

Long, sensual strokes alternated with short, deep thrusts of his fingers into her tender muscles. "You surprised me tonight," he said.

"You mean you aren't used to being mauled by women?" Sam held no illusions. He might have taken charge, but she had definitely *approached* him first.

He laughed. "I was talking about you helping out around here. You pitched in when I needed it most. I appreciate it."

His hands had moved higher, working their way up her thigh. She tensed, but under his continued ministrations, she began to relax again and enjoy.

"I can pay you Theresa's salary," he said.

"You already paid Theresa her salary," she reminded him.

"Because her family needs the money and Bear won't mind. You don't need to work for free. It isn't much, but…"

Sam could barely concentrate on anything but the feel of his hands on her bare skin and the thought of where they were headed next. But through the tingling sensations and the desire, she got a solid view of Mac. A special, caring man…hers for the duration of her stay, if she wanted him to be. And she did.

In return, he needed to know what she wanted from him, and that didn't include cash. "I don't want your money, Mac."

He muttered something she almost missed. Something that sounded like "That would be a first," but his agile fingers had reached the hem of her skirt and she knew she couldn't trust anything she heard except her own rapid breathing.

"Why not?" he asked. "You earned it."

"I don't take payment for things I enjoy, and I enjoyed helping you."

"I'm sure you picked up a lot in tips tonight, anyway," he said.

"I didn't do too badly for my first night." She grinned.

"You're a hell of a woman, Sammy Jo." His drawl was deliberate, she knew, as was the way his finger dipped beneath the lace in her panties. At that first intimate touch, she let out a slow moan, accompanied by a tremor her body couldn't control.

"Is this the way you show your gratitude?" she asked, trying to keep the moment between them light even as his finger moved over the lace, rubbing back and forth with unerring accuracy. It didn't work. Fire shot straight through her body, making her burn.

"No, sweetheart. I'm doing this because it turns you on and *I* enjoy that." To her disappointment, though, he slipped his fingers out from beneath her skirt. His hand shook as he placed it on her thigh. That telling gesture made his withdrawal easier to take. She wasn't alone in this swirling, all-encompassing state of desire.

"But I want you wide awake and participating, not exhausted from working behind the bar." He placed a gentle kiss on her lips before bending to retrieve her shoes.

"Go on up and I'll meet you after I've cleaned up."

Sam blinked, her mind unable to comprehend his words because her body was strung so tight she thought she might explode. She could attempt to seduce him, but she didn't want their first time to be in the bar.

Despite her inexperienced technique, she'd made it this far. She was more than content to let him take the lead. As she offered a wave and headed for the stairs, she realized Mac was right. She was exhausted. From the look of things down here, he might be a while and she could put the time to good use. After she relaxed, she would set exactly the right mood.

MAC HIT THE TOP STEP at a run. When was the last time he had a woman he'd invited warming his bed? Okay, not his bed, but he'd make do. Because not only did he like what he saw, but he liked what he'd learned about her, too. She wasn't selfish and greedy, but considerate and giving beyond belief. Not only to Mac when he needed a hand, but to Zee and the other regular customers, who made it a point to mention how much they liked his new waitress. She fit in, which surprised him, considering he'd bet his last dollar she'd never waited tables in her life.

They generated such instant and spontaneous combustion, it was hard to believe he'd only known Samantha for a couple of hours. When he opened the door, he walked into a candlelit room. He had to give her credit for ingenuity. She must have snuck back downstairs while he was cleaning and swiped the red candle holders from the tables. Thick white candles flickered in the darkness, casting a muted glow, creating a sexy atmosphere.

Mac's gaze went straight for the bed to see what other surprises awaited him. Samantha had crawled on top of the covers fully dressed, cuddled up with one pillow...and had fallen fast asleep.

His gaze fell on her sleeping form. Light from the candles shimmered over her face, drawing his attention to her delicate profile, high cheekbones and full lips. Lips he'd like to sample again. It wouldn't be happening, he thought, watching the slow rise and fall of her chest. Which was a good thing, considering he'd promised himself to take things slowly and read the subtle signs she gave out. Not the overt ones, like the candlelit room decorated for seduction.

He eased himself beside her on the bed and tucked a wayward strand of hair off her cheek. She sighed softly and cuddled close to him. Interesting how she instinctively went toward him, even at her most defenseless. His heart gave a lurch.

In sleep, she looked more lost than she had when she'd wandered into the bar. Judging from the trouble she'd gone to setting up this seduction, he sensed, as he had earlier, that she considered a sexual encounter an answer to her problems. It would be too easy to succumb to temptation and take what she offered. If he did, he'd never see her again.

Mac didn't know how he knew this to be true. He just did. Losing Samantha before he got to know her wasn't an option. For now, he would take care of her and give her time to confide in him. Even if he had to sit on his hands and pray, he'd damn well do his best not to muddy the waters with sex. At least not yet.

Her eyelashes fluttered against her soft skin and she murmured to herself in her sleep. A bad dream? Mac pressed a kiss to her forehead, ignoring the throbbing in his groin brought on by even that innocent touch. Because more than he wanted her, he wished he could make whatever she was running from go away.

He wasn't anybody's white knight, and he didn't normally look for the nearest damsel in distress to rescue. But he wanted to protect *this woman*. He wanted to take care of Samantha. Mac didn't question why. He had a week to find out.

WHEN HIS INTERNAL CLOCK woke him early the next morning, he realized he hadn't slept much at all. How could he with Samantha's small but firm body tucked into his and her hand wrapped around a morning erection that had nothing to do with the time of day and everything to do with the woman beside him?

Good intentions aside, he'd gone to bed wanting her and awakened wanting her even more. Last night's erotic episode after closing stayed with him. He could still recall her moist heat against his fingertips and could easily envision his body sliding into hers. The soft noises coming from beside him told him she slept soundly, which put off the inevitable test of his resolve.

With a groan, he rolled over and dragged himself out of bed. He couldn't help but glance back once more. She'd rolled to his side of the bed and wrapped herself around a pillow. His pillow. And damned if she didn't look like she belonged there.

Mac shook his head. A cold shower would take care of his problem at least temporarily. It would also clear his mind to face the start of his week with Samantha.

SAM WAITED UNTIL SHE HEARD the bathroom door closing behind Mac before flipping onto her back and opening her eyes. An arousing masculine scent filled her nostrils at the same time the sound of running water reached her ears. Mac's scent, Mac's shower. The same Mac she'd avoided this morning after awakening with her hand wrapped around his…his… She couldn't even think the word, let alone utter it aloud.

She forced herself to sit up and glanced around the room. Sunlight filtered through the blinds, and the candles she'd lit earlier had burned or been snuffed out. She glanced at a small bedside clock. The gleaming digital numbers told her she'd slept past her normal 7:00 a.m. wake-up time. Long past. Apparently bartenders had to alter their internal clocks to conform to late hours. She'd have to adjust, at least for the week. While she was with Mac.

She took another look around and cringed. She'd fallen asleep before he'd come up last night, and as a result, she'd awakened to face a failed seduction attempt. Mortified, she hadn't been able to make the first move, other than the unconscious one. Given the fact that she'd felt him pulsing against her palm, hard, warm and very male, she'd counted on him to act first. Obviously he had other plans.

She ought to be grateful she'd slept through making a complete fool of herself. Sam tossed the covers off. If she was dressed and out of the apartment before he finished his shower, she'd give herself some time to think. Her mind always worked better when she was outdoors, and with the fresh air and open spaces Arizona offered, she'd probably figure out how to handle a man like Mac in no time.

Bending down, she pulled out a cream-and-peach-flowered sundress and laid it out on the bed. She tipped her head to the side. The shower still pulsed in the background. So did the beat of music she no longer had to strain to hear.

The refrain sounded throughout the bedroom and she couldn't suppress a grin. So he liked music when he showered, she mused. She now knew one more thing about Mac. The thought pleased her. So did the fact that they shared the same taste in music. Her hips swayed to the country-and-western beat as she pulled her shirt over her head and shook her hair out behind her.

The jarring sound of a door opening startled her from the easy rhythm of the music. Unthinking, she whirled toward the sound, only to find herself facing Mac, bare-chested with a towel wrapped around his waist and nothing more.

"You've got rhythm," he said with a grin.

She felt burning heat rise to her cheeks. Water dripped over his bronzed skin. Her fingertips itched to follow the same path. "The shower's still running," she said inanely.

"Forgot my razor. It's new." He stepped toward the wooden dresser at the same time she made a dive for her clothes. The man was destined to see her at her worst, she thought, struggling to pull the soft cotton over her exposed breasts.

Clothed, but nowhere near composed, she turned back toward him. He studied her with an inscrutable expression, but there was one thing she couldn't mistake—the burning desire in his gaze.

She swallowed hard, then forced a smile. "Have everything you need?" she asked, careful to keep her gaze at eye level. Away from the towel that rode low on his hips, revealing a tan line and a swell of passion she couldn't mistake.

"Not nearly," he muttered.

She licked her lips, not knowing how to answer that.

"As long as you're up, I thought I'd take you out, get you a decent breakfast. There's nothing good in the refrigerator downstairs," he said.

She blinked, stunned by the absurd intimacy of the situation. She and Mac were sharing a morning routine and comfortable conversation while they were both barely dressed. They were strangers, for heaven's sake.

Her mind and her heart shouted in denial. They might have met only yesterday, but she and Mac were far from strangers. She felt too comfortable in his presence, too safe in his arms. The realization shook her composure.

She didn't know if she could get food into her nervous stomach, but a trip away from the bar and these close quarters seemed like an excellent idea.

SHE WASN'T WEARING A BRA. Not unless she put one on when he'd gone downstairs to give her a minute or two of privacy. Mac gripped the steering wheel, his fists clenched as hard and as tight as his body. This morning's shock still hadn't worn off. He'd stepped out to find Samantha half-naked, her body bracketed by sunlight, her dark hair falling against the white skin of her back. And then when she'd turned around…all his good intentions had nearly been shot to hell right then and there.

When his choices had come down to tossing her onto the bed or tossing her onto the bed, he knew he was in trouble. Breakfast in a restaurant, sitting across from each other in a decent-size booth, had seemed like a good way to take the edge off the escalating sexual tension between them. He'd been wrong.

She'd sat across from him wearing the dress she'd grabbed earlier, and all he could think of was her full breasts as they'd looked before she'd managed to run for cover. Even now, as he drove through the countryside, he couldn't think of anything else. She'd asked him to detour and show her the sights on their way back to the bar. That, too, had seemed like a good idea at the time. But considering his current train of thought, he wasn't sure Arizona's rock formations would take his mind off Samantha.

He needed to give her space. He wanted all the time her week with him would allow, but there was no way he could continue to keep his hands to himself if she tempted him at every turn. Even her graceful hand movements aroused him.

"Mac, stop!"

He slammed on the brakes, nearly sending them into a skid. He didn't know if he was more on edge from inhaling her scent in the confines of the small car, or from thinking about her incredible body and what he'd like to do with it. The car screeched to a halt and he shoved the gear shift to Park. Luckily, they'd hopped onto a back road that was rarely used.

He darted a worried glance at Samantha.

"You stopped. I didn't think you'd take me literally."

"When someone screams in a car, I figure they're either going to be sick or they have to…" He shook his head. "Never mind. What's the emergency?"

Looking sheepish, she asked, "What's the little village over there?" She pointed to the scenic cluster of shops and stores in the distance. A panoramic picture of arches and rooftops painted in a variety of pinks, greens and light browns rose against the blue sky.

"That's a small place called Cave Cove. A tourist trap with Indian dolls, T-shirts, turquoise jewelry and other southwestern stuff you easterners like to bring home." Despite the commercialism, the place brought money into the town's economy and provided jobs for the locals. Mac wasn't a shopper himself, but his sister and mother always picked up unique pieces in the small stores during each of their monthly visits.

He shifted gears, intending to continue toward their destination, when her warm hand on his arm stopped him.

"Could we go there first?"

"If you want a mall, there's an upscale place back in Scottsdale." Which he hated, but for her, he'd force himself to endure it.

"A large indoor mall? Air-conditioned so I can freeze?" She rubbed her arms at the thought. "Expensive shops and obnoxious sales help? No, thanks. I get my fill of that back home."

He'd just bet she did. From what he'd seen of her clothing so far, everything had designer tags or labels, similar to the type of things the shops stocked at The Resort. No doubt she frequented similar upscale places in whatever state she did her shopping.

He glanced over. She'd crinkled up her nose in distaste. Samantha dressed well and looked gorgeous, but she obviously didn't enjoy the process, nor did she make it her life's work

"You sure you want to stop there?" he asked.

"I'd really like to take a look around. Please?" She peeked up at him through wide eyes and batted those lashes in a move she still hadn't quite perfected.

He laughed hard. "Okay, we'll hit the stores and save the sights for later."

"Do you think they have those little dolls? Because I promised myself I'd pick one up while I'm here."

"I know for a fact they do." Thanks to his sister's collection. If he ever brought Samantha with him to Sedona, his mother and sister would take to her immediately.

Whoa. Mac stopped himself. It was one thing to think about a lifetime commitment in the abstract, but it was a whole different story for him to think of Samantha being accepted by his female family members. Although she would be. He knew it as certainly as he knew Samantha would accept them.

He glanced over. She'd perched her sunglasses on top of her head in an unconscious move that was as honest as it was erotic. Even her everyday movements tantalized him.

She rested her forehead against the car window and gazed longingly toward the quaint town. "It's incredibly beautiful here," she said quietly.

"It is, isn't it?" These surroundings were as much a part of him as his blood, but he never took them for granted. He hadn't grown up wealthy. When money came later on, a man tended to appreciate all he had. Mac did. He glanced at Samantha once more. And when he found what he wanted, he didn't let go.

"Peaceful," Sam said. "No skyscrapers, no smog, no bumper-to-bumper traffic or blaring car horns."

He hummed the theme song to *Jeopardy* before answering, "What is…New York City?"

She laughed. "You could have just asked where I'm from."

"You live there?"

"Work there. I commute from New Jersey, forty minutes a day."

"Why?"

She looked out the window. Mountains provided a backdrop for a wide variety of cacti and plant life. Looking at the sun overhead, a bright ball of fire in an otherwise clear blue sky, she shook her head. "I have no idea. I was born and raised there, so I stayed, I guess. Plus financial planners do best in New York. What about you?"

"An Arizona native."

"So you have family here?"

He nodded. "Mother and sister, a brother-in-law and a six-month-old nephew."

She didn't like thinking about him as a man with family, people who loved and cared about him. Somehow that made him too real, too unforgettable.

"What about you?" he asked. "Any family?"

"Just my dad."

His understanding groan filled the small car. "What happened?"

"My mother passed away a couple of years ago... and..."

"And?" he prodded when she remained silent.

"Dad didn't cope well. He's a stockbroker and works for one of the big brokerage firms in the city." And of course, Sam, in her quest for parental approval, had gone into financial planning, a similar field, to emulate her father and make him proud. She was never quite sure she'd accomplished her goal, so it was a good thing she loved her choice of careers.

She sighed. "First he neglected his clients, then he tried to compensate. I didn't know until recently, but in the last year, Dad's been dipping into high-risk stocks and losing a lot of money. His boss wasn't pleased when several of his clients took their business elsewhere. Both his professional and personal portfolios are a mess. The worse things got, the more time he spent doing anything but watching the market…." She cut herself off with a laugh.

Tipping her head to the side, she met his gaze. "You're easy to talk to, you know that?"

"Then keep going." He lay a hand on her arm, and she let the warmth seep through her.

"If you're sure you want to hear."

Dark eyes reassured her. "I do."

"He's nearly broke. I should have seen it coming, but I didn't." And considering the solution, oh, how she wished she had. Sam shook her head. "I was so busy with my own life and job that I didn't realize what was going on. By the time I did, he'd not only fallen into serious debt, he'd lost most of his long-standing clients."

His hand moved from her arm to her fingers as he cupped her hand in a gentle grip.

"You can't control his life for him."

"No, but I'm not so sure he can, either. At first I thought it was a grief-induced lapse and he'd snap out of it. But now I think he's just getting older and less meticulous, more forgetful, maybe. If I'd paid more attention…"

"You aren't responsible for your father's actions."

She raised an eyebrow. If only he knew. "I promised my mother I'd take care of him," she explained. Problem was, her dying mother had envisioned Sam teaching him to use the washing machine, not giving up her own freedom to ensure her father didn't lose the house or his status in the community.

"Besides, I've always done the right thing," she murmured. Always sought her parents' approval… their elusive affection. She'd found both at the time her mother had passed away. She loved her father and wanted to help. But everything she wanted would now cost her dearly. She tipped her head for a glance at Mac.

"I can understand that kind of vow," he said. "I promised my father the same thing."

Too real, too unforgettable. She drew a shuddering breath. This morning would have been the perfect time to escape, before she got to know him, before she got to like him.

But since it was too late for that, Sam decided she wanted his understanding as well. "So you can see how a promise can change your whole life…" She stopped herself before she revealed too much, realizing how honest she'd been and how dangerous the level of emotional intimacy had become.

This week wasn't reality, she reminded herself. It was a sliver of time that belonged to her and Mac alone. She had no business bringing her real life into the picture, as if he were someone she could confide in. Someone who would be around when all was said and done. Because no matter how much she grew to like him, no matter how much she might care, Samantha had to walk away. Regardless of how painful it might be.

She'd be hurting him, too, and that thought bothered her most of all. She wrapped her free arm around herself to ward off the unwanted chill, a chill that came from deep inside her.

As if sensing the conversation had ended and respecting her silence, he shifted to Drive and pulled back onto the road. Her other hand remained safe in his, his touch warm and comforting on her skin. "I'm sorry about your mother," he told her, his gaze fixed ahead. "And I know that any solution to your father's problems will be tough on you. Be there for him, advise him, and help him if you can. But remember, you can't give up the rest of your life because he's having trouble with his."

If he only knew. She slid her gaze to the window,

unable to look at him. Although he knew she was leaving for the conference next week, he had no idea how final their goodbyes would truly be.

CHAPTER FOUR

MAC DROVE INTO TOWN and parallel-parked on a small side street in front of a store painted in bright colors with warm, welcoming signs in each window. He'd no sooner turned off the ignition than Sam jumped out of the car and onto the sidewalk. Mac joined her as she stared into a window filled with T-shirts in a variety of sizes and colors. He slipped his hand into hers and they made their way through the town, stopping to browse in various shops. Just being by his side gave her a renewed sense of warmth and happiness she'd never known before.

Being an only child, she'd never had brothers or sisters to run and play with while her parents walked hand in hand. She'd always felt the loss. Always been an outsider in her own life. Until now. She shivered despite the warm sun overhead. Now was not the time to be finding things in life that satisfied her unless they were memories to be stored and cherished. Her time with Mac was certainly that.

Benches lined the street, along with old lamps and chipped painted signs. He'd been smart to suggest this outing. She'd needed to get away from the bar for a while, not to mention escaping the sizzling sexual tension that seemed never to be far from the surface. Cave Cove sported every kind of tourist shop imaginable. And here, in the outdoors, she was able to relax, to enjoy the day and Mac without pressure.

The town was empty because of the early hour, so they had the streets and shops to themselves. At the end of the sidewalk, she came to a small jewelry store with a hand-carved wooden sign out front. Turquoise-and-silver jewelry was beautifully displayed in a window setting. She paused outside.

He tugged lightly on her hand. "Let's keep walking. There are tons of stores with the same things in all these little alleyways."

A large red sign inside caught her eye. "But this one is offering thirty percent off."

He laughed. "Every jewelry store here offers thirty percent off. Competition. They couldn't stay in business otherwise. It's a gimmick designed to get people like you inside."

She placed her palms on the cool glass. Something about the dangling glass reflectors and wind chimes hanging from the ceiling called to her. "This is the place," she insisted.

"If you say so. Just remember there's plenty of landmarks you'll miss if you spend all your time here."

She frowned. "You mean you're getting bored already."

"Did I say that?" He had the audacity to look insulted.

"It's a well-known fact that men hate shopping."

"A statistic I'm proud to say I'm a part of. But not today. Come on." Keeping her hand tucked in his, he led her inside.

Bells tinkled as they entered a shop smelling of lavender potpourri. Goose bumps prickled along her skin and she shivered, causing Mac to draw her closer and wrap his strong arm around her waist. A strange sensation she couldn't name enveloped her. If she believed in auras and premonitions, she would think she'd reached a turning point in her life. That any decision she made now would chart the course of her future. Silly, considering she didn't believe in any of those things.

Shaking off the ridiculous notion, she walked to the nearest jewelry case and studied the rings. Though the display was filled, one in particular caught her eye. A band of silver, crisscrossed with turquoise...

"See anything you like?" a female voice asked.

Sam looked up. Thanks to her internal musings, she'd been expecting a gypsylike woman cloaked in veils and mystery instead of the chic older woman who greeted her.

When she didn't answer right away, Mac nudged her arm. "Sweetheart?"

She started at his use of the intimate name in public. "Yes, sorry." She tapped the glass case. "That one. The one in the shape of an X."

The silver-haired woman smiled. "Aah, The Kiss." As she spoke, she pulled a black velvet box filled with assorted rings from the case. "I'd like to say it's an original, but I commission another each time I sell this to engaged couples like yourselves."

Sam waited for Mac to correct the woman's assumption. When he didn't, she started to do it herself. "We're not…"

"Sure we're ready to buy yet," he said smoothly. "Especially a ring that so many other women are wearing." She tipped her head and sent him a questioning glance. She looked into his eyes. Eyes that were sincere, calming, loving. *Loving?*

Sam wanted to run from the store in a panic, and she would have if Mac hadn't placed a firm hand on her arm. Swallowing hard, she dared another glance at his face. This time he winked, then leaned down to whisper in her ear. "This week is a time for fantasies. Indulge me."

She didn't know whether to laugh because he was

joking or cry because she wished she were free to think of this man in terms of love and marriage.

Apparently taking their silence as indecision, the shopkeeper spoke. "You can rest assured, as long as you wear this ring, you will be wed for eternity. Every other couple who purchased it can attest to the same."

That feeling, that…aura swept over Sam once again and she trembled. "What makes you so sure we're engaged?" she felt compelled to ask. There was no ring on her finger, nor any suntan line where Tom's ring had once been.

"I recognize the signs. The closeness…" She gestured to Mac's hand, draped possessively over Sam's shoulder. "The way he looks at you when he thinks you aren't looking, the way you curl into him…two halves make a whole," she said.

"You don't look like a gypsy fortune-teller," Sam muttered.

Mac laughed. "Give the lady a break, Sammy Jo. You want the ring or not?"

Without waiting for an answer, he reached into his pocket and withdrew a credit card. Sam dared a glance, catching only the last name, Mackenzie, before he handed the worn plastic to the obviously pleased woman. So Mackenzie, *Mac,* was his last name. Another thing she'd learned about him, she thought, storing the information away with the rest of her memories.

"Excuse us," Sam said to the salesclerk. "And please hold off a minute before ringing that up."

She led Mac to a secluded corner of the store. "About the ring…"

"You changed your mind?"

"No, but…"

"You want to try it on first. I should have realized."

"No, I mean…" She didn't know how to broach this without offending him, but she knew he was a bartender and… "You didn't even ask the price."

"I didn't have to. I saw the look in your eye the minute you saw the ring."

"But, Mac…"

He treated her to his sexy grin, meant to turn her on and melt her mind so she couldn't think. The throbbing heat low down in her stomach told her he'd managed the first. She opened her mouth to argue.

"It's thirty percent off," he reminded her. "How expensive could it be? Let me do this one thing for you…Sammy Jo."

Her new nickname, especially on *his* lips, had begun to grow on her. So did the way his voice dropped an octave when he said it in that husky tone. Gazing into his eyes, she could see how much this meant to him, and she couldn't bring herself to turn him down. A quick try would satisfy them both. Her ring size was unusually small, and the thin silver couldn't be sized easily. She'd have an excuse to refuse it without offending his pride.

They walked back to the counter where the ring waited on a black velvet liner. She looked around, but the salesclerk had disappeared into the back room, leaving them alone. "Trusting," Sam murmured.

"This isn't the city, sweetheart."

He picked up the ring and lifted her hand. "Whenever you look at this ring, think about me, this week, and what could be."

Before she could protest, he'd slipped the ring on her left hand, braced her face in his palms and lowered his head for a kiss. She tipped her head back, moaning as his lips played over hers in a gentle, coaxing motion. He bit gently on her lower lip and she opened at his command, letting his tongue dart inside and possess hers. Sam didn't know where fantasy began or reality left off. As long as Mac held her, touched and kissed her, as long as he treated her as if he loved her, she didn't care.

He raised his head and smiled. She looked into his eyes and her heart leaped in her chest. She'd offend his pride more by rejecting the gift than by letting him pay for it. "Thank you," she murmured.

"My pleasure." His hand went to hers as he lifted her finger. "A perfect fit."

She glanced down, amazed. "Sometimes you get lucky."

"Yes, you do." His gaze bore into hers. She was struck by the intensity she saw there before it quickly disappeared. "Ready to hit the road again?" he asked.

Was he trying to disarm her? If so, it was working. By giving her a glimpse of the generous man inside the sexy male body, he'd managed to charm her as well. She might not know details about the way he lived, but she was beginning to think she knew him in the ways that counted.

Enough for little doubts about the rest of her life to begin creeping in. She pushed them aside in favor of more practical considerations. "How far are we from the bar?" she asked.

"Another half an hour. Why?"

"I'm starving."

"You can't be hungry for food? We just ate."

"What else is there?" She laughed, but when she met his darkened gaze, the laughter died on her lips. She realized exactly what he desired. Her body understood and reacted. A tingling in her abdomen, a tightening in her breasts, and a soul-deep longing grew near her heart.

"Zee left his special chili in the refrigerator at the bar. Do you like it hot?" His voice resembled a growl.

She swallowed over the lump that had formed in her throat. "Very," she managed to say, thanking her lucky stars they were in a public place.

He exhaled a harsh groan. "Know what I like most about you?"

"My big heart?"

He grabbed her hand. The heat shot straight down to her toes. "Your even bigger stomach."

She smiled. "Food's an important consideration. You can't survive without it, you know."

His chuckle vibrated deep from his chest. "I know."

She waited while he signed and pocketed the credit card receipt, forcing deep, even breaths into her chest. They walked to the car, his ring on her finger and her hand tucked inside his.

Although desire was constantly sizzling beneath the surface, easy banter between them came naturally. How many long-married couples could claim both?

When she was with Mac, contentment filled her, but she knew it couldn't last. Which was why she had to keep reminding herself that their time together was nothing more than a fantasy. What else would she call a gypsy woman's promise that couldn't possibly come true?

SHE STOOD BEHIND THE BAR, filling wooden bowls with nachos and dip, preparing for the night ahead. The lady was hotter than the salsa she poured, and to her credit, she had no idea. Saturday already. Time was slipping by fast.

Last night had been a typical Friday at The Hungry Bear—busy, hectic and generally insane. Samantha hadn't complained, merely pitched in and worked until closing, while Mac had spent the evening watching and wondering. She hadn't changed out of that damn dress, and though it hung to her ankles, it emphasized every subtle curve.

Not knowing if she wore a bra beneath the flowered fabric nearly did him in. The men at The Hungry Bear weren't blind and Samantha was new to these parts. That alone made her a point of interest. He wondered if they, too, were watching the rise and fall of her breasts as she worked. He'd spent half the damn night wiping the sweat off his forehead and reminding himself he'd promised restraint.

Which wasn't easy, considering she made sure she touched him each time she passed. Even if she hadn't, he'd catch a whiff of peaches. Her seductive scent stood out in the bar.

Then she passed out cold before he ever made it upstairs. Mac understood. Being on her feet all night was grueling for anyone, especially a novice. After a restless night's sleep, he'd awakened on Saturday close to noon. Samantha had still been out cold. So he'd used the time to head on over to The Resort and check in, making it back to The Hungry Bear in time for opening, bags of tortillas in hand.

She hadn't questioned his absence and he hadn't

felt obligated to explain. Yet another thing he received from Samantha. Unconditional trust and understanding. He wondered how she'd take it when he told her the truth.

She'd forgive him. Although the body and beautiful face had attracted him first, her lack of awareness and pretense interested him most. She'd understand him. She had from the first.

Just as he understood her. The tired woman who pitched in behind the bar, the sensitive woman who'd confided in him, the woman with deep familial feelings and values, she had made the biggest impression. Not that he'd forgotten the supple curves beneath his hands, or her unabashed response to his touch. But so much more than the packaging appealed to him now.

Their outing yesterday had been a mistake. He hadn't given himself distance, he'd drawn himself in deeper. Every time he turned around, Samantha was there…in his thoughts, his dreams…his future?

All last night, he'd sensed her approach as she passed beside him, her hip brushing against him, her scent wrapping itself around him. How the hell was he supposed to keep his distance if she kept up the innocent touches, the soft laughter, or the inane questions about customers that had them sharing what seemed like intimate jokes.

Mac couldn't stand another minute. Coming up behind her, he grabbed her around the waist.

"Oh!" She jumped back into his chest before easing herself into him. "Don't sneak up on me like that."

"Why not? I get to hold you this way."

She turned in his arms, looping her hands around his neck. "You get to hold me any way."

He liked that thought. "I called Theresa, and there's no way she can make it in tonight."

"So?" She reached for a nacho and took a bite, then held the chip up to his mouth.

He finished it off, licking the salt off his lips and taking a nip at her finger as well. A small bite, but enough to make her eyes glaze with desire. He grinned. "So I'm shorthanded again."

Stepping backward, she held her arms out before him. "What are these, if not two very willing hands?" She slipped those hands beneath his shirt and placed her palms on his chest. With yesterday's confidences behind them, Samantha seemed to feel more comfortable around him. He let himself enjoy the free-spirited part of her nature.

"You're on vacation," he said through gritted teeth. Her warm hands against his flesh aroused him beyond belief.

"Define vacation."

"A break from reality, doing what you enjoy."

"Exactly." Her fingernails raked lightly against his chest. "Working in this bar is a break from nine-to-five corporate reality." She raised his shirt and pressed her lips to his skin. "And touching you is something I definitely enjoy." Her tongue darted out and back, tasting him briefly before she raised her gaze. "Unless you don't like it?"

She asked as if she really didn't know. The innocent asserting herself again. The woman was making keeping his promise to himself more difficult with each passing minute. He didn't know how much longer he could keep his hands off her. He let out a ragged groan.

"I guess you do." She treated him to a soft but sexy smile.

He'd wanted her before, but the feelings she inspired now were incredible. If the bar wasn't opening for business in fifteen minutes, he might lose his last shred of self-control. He wanted their first time to be someplace better than a tabletop in The Hungry Bear. A soft bed and plenty of lingering time was what he had in mind.

He pushed his hand through her hair, bringing her face within inches of his own. Just a kiss. A quick taste of her glossy lips. He bent his head and got a heady, moist taste… Just as a loud banging sound came from the bar door.

"Open up." When he got no immediate response, Zee yelled. "Dammit, Mac, I lost my key."

"The old man knows we're shorthanded. Probably thinks he's here to help."

Her face had turned a deep shade of red, and she pulled his shirt back down. Zee's distinctive cackle didn't help the situation. "Well he could have called first," she muttered.

He shot her an amused glance. "We're open in a few minutes," he reminded her.

"I'm going upstairs to wash up," she said. "I'll be back."

He gave Samantha time to disappear up the back stairs before calling out to Zee. "Hang on, I'm coming," Mac yelled. He pulled on his T-shirt and tucked it back into the waistband of his jeans. The insistent pounding continued even as Mac flipped the dead bolt and yanked open the door.

"We're still closed even for you."

Zee ignored him and walked inside. "I've known you all your life, Mackenzie. Don't pull any of that high-and-mighty crap on me."

Mac rolled his eyes. So the old man had been his father's best friend and a part of Mac's life for as long as he could remember. That didn't give him the right to interrupt his sex life and drive him generally insane. This place belonged to Bear, though, which gave the old man more right to be here than Mac. And he did love the codger like a father.

He followed Zee to a bar stool and sat down.

"Where's your lady friend?" Zee asked.

"You scared her off."

"Hah. Maybe she got smart and went to a hotel."

Mac leaned on an elbow. "If you want to know something, just ask."

"I did. Where's your lady friend?"

He groaned. "Upstairs."

"That's what I thought." Zee smacked Mac in the shoulder. "Didn't your daddy and I teach you boys anything? First my dumb son lets a woman give him the runaround, and then there's you."

"What the hell did I do?"

"In my day, a man married a woman before he took her to bed. I understand those rules don't apply today, but dammit boy, how about a little romance before you sleep with her?"

"I didn't sleep with her." Yet. He'd slept next to her, though, and Zee wouldn't approve of that, either. Mac let out another groan. He was thirty-five. His own father had died twelve years ago, and Zee had stepped in without asking, guiding him through every rough patch in his life. He always seemed to pop up whenever Mac needed a father's advice.

He didn't recall asking for that right now, but he respected Zee enough to listen and think about what the old man said.

"I don't want any of the gory details," Zee muttered. "I can see enough without 'em." His probing blue gaze settled on Mac's face. "Wipe the damn makeup off your lips. You look like a pansy."

Mac muttered a succinct curse and rubbed his lips with a paper napkin.

Zee shook his head. "I just want you to think with your brain and not your... Well, you know what I mean."

"You made your point."

"So is she any good?"

Mac let out a hearty chuckle. "Now, that's the Zee I expected."

The old man reached for one of the bowls Samantha had filled earlier. "She must be if you haven't given her the boot yet." A loud crunching sounded in Mac's ear.

"Gentlemen don't kiss and tell. Your rule."

"No, that one belonged to your daddy. I revealed plenty. The only way to corner Bear's mama into marrying me was by ruining her reputation." He grinned. "So you tell Sammy Jo the truth yet?"

"No." The answer earned Mac another swat in the shoulder. "She's from New Jersey," Mac said. As if that explained anything.

For the first time, he let himself think about the fact that not only would Samantha leave in a few days for her conference, but she had a life and a father who needed her back East. A strange emptiness accompanied the admission, one he knew he'd have to deal with, and soon.

Zee shrugged. "Heck, I thought the Wright boys invented the airplane."

"You're hilarious," Mac said. He wasn't ready to deal with a long-distance relationship any more than he was ready to reveal his feelings for Samantha to Zee. "I met the woman less than forty-eight hours ago." Funny, but it felt as if he'd known her much longer. "I barely know her." Yet he'd been more intimate with her without the benefit of sex than with any other woman he'd known.

"So why not level with her? Afraid she'll run the other way if she knows you're too wealthy for us mere mortals?"

"Actually, I'm more afraid she won't."

"Aah." Zee placed an understanding arm on Mac's shoulder. "I figured that was why you never picked up one of them spa bunnies. That's no excuse for not introducing me to one of 'em, but I'll forgive you."

Mac grinned. "And now I feel much better."

"When's she going back?" Zee asked.

Mac felt his smile turn to a frown. "Soon enough." Unless he changed her mind. He rose from his seat. "Just forget about it," he said to the well-meaning older man.

"I will…if you can do the same once she's gone."

He was about to respond, when the sound of footsteps running down the stairs stopped him. Unwilling to embarrass Samantha further, Mac crumpled the napkin and tossed it into the trash beneath the bar. Zee's knowing cackle followed his movement.

She cleared her throat, and Mac turned to see her standing beside him, dressed in a soft pink T-shirt, tight jeans and a matching bandanna threaded through the belt loops. Her hair fell over her shoulder, a soft smile touched her lips, and Mac knew he was in deep.

Things between them had shifted, and he wondered if he'd ever reclaim level ground.

SAM CLASPED HER HANDS together in front of her. The ring shone on her finger, a reminder of how close she and Mac had become. Their trip hadn't given her time to think. Neither had his absence today. She hadn't learned how to handle him, just the opposite. She'd grown to care for this man who was supposed to be passing through her life.

A life that until now had been dull in the extreme. She was approaching thirty, had lived an ordinary life, held an ordinary job and had dated ordinary men who she'd had little interest in becoming intimate with. She'd done the obligatory thing, seeing co-workers and allowing friends to set her up. She'd even slept with one man who had lasted beyond the awkward dating stage, one she'd hoped she could care for, but things had fizzled fast. Even then, she had never, ever contemplated the intimacy she craved with Mac.

True, she'd come out here seeking excitement, but her emotions were never supposed to come into play. He'd broken many barriers, she thought, fingering the token of his…what? Friendship, certainly. Affection? She met his gaze, and he treated her to a wink before continuing his conversation with Zee. The flutters in her stomach increased until she thought she might jump out of her skin. She didn't dare name anything else.

Each time she even looked at Mac, another emotional wall fell. She'd come to Arizona seeking passion, and she'd found it without even sleeping with him. Heaven help her when his body eventually did fuse with hers.

The churning in her stomach gave her a clue. How was that possible? How could her body crave him with such intensity, as if it knew what awaited her in Mac's arms?

"Hey, you okay?" Mac's warm hand touched her arm as he walked up to her.

She met his concerned gaze and forced a smile. "Couldn't be better. The bar opens in less than five minutes. I've got my sneakers on and I'm ready to work."

"That wasn't what I meant."

"I know what you meant." Reaching over, she touched a trembling hand to his still damp lips.

Surely passion that burned so strong would douse itself soon.

Still, she couldn't help but wonder how she'd live
the rest of her life without him if it didn't.

CHAPTER FIVE

HE'D TAKEN HIS TIME stacking the stools onto the tables. The glass top of the long bar now sparkled and shone. If he washed the bar glasses any slower, he'd collapse from the sheer boredom of the task. Mac glanced at his watch. Surely Samantha had fallen asleep by now.

The only way he could trust himself to strip down to his briefs and climb into that small double bed beside her, was to make sure she was out for the night. His patience was near to breaking, but he drew the line at taking advantage of a comatose woman.

He'd like nothing better than to rouse Samantha from sleep with erotic whisperings in her ear and sensual strokes of his hand. Unfortunately, she wasn't ready. She might be free with her touches... and her tongue, he thought wryly. His body was on fire just thinking about her dainty licks against his chest. But the hesitancy wasn't gone from her gaze, the tremors still evident in her touch.

Mac might have been selective over the past couple of years, but he knew women. An experienced female who knew what she desired didn't hesitate to take what she wanted. Samantha did. He still believed she saw sex as the answer to...whatever she'd left behind at home. Mac didn't. Hanging out in the bar was the only way he could guarantee that he kept his hands to himself.

He leaned down to put a rag beneath the bar and found an envelope with Theresa's name and the word *tips* scrawled beneath. Mac drew in a deep breath. Just when he thought he knew Samantha, she stunned him even more. Caring was as much a part of her as her innate sensuality.

He exhaled hard. Oh, yeah. Hanging out in the bar was definitely his safest bet.

SAM SAT UP IN BED. For the third morning in a row, she awoke to the sun forcing its way through the blinds, the sound of the shower in her ears, and country music reverberating throughout the room. For the third morning in a row, she woke up alone.

It was ironic, really. She'd come west intent on seducing a man, and here she'd had Mac to herself for three whole days and he hadn't made one move to take her to bed.

Oh, he'd slept with her, all right. But that's all he did. He worked so hard after hours, she couldn't manage to stay awake until he walked up the stairs...

and she'd tried. To add insult to injury, he beat her out of bed every morning, and it didn't matter that she'd woken up earlier each day.

She didn't doubt his interest. She couldn't. Between his sultry looks and his heated touch, she knew he wanted her. She glanced toward the closed bathroom door and bit down on her lower lip. Her body couldn't stand another second of deprivation. But that wasn't the only reason she had to approach Mac, and she had to do it now. Before she lost her nerve.

She'd come here to have a steamy sexual encounter. Instead she'd found Mac. A sensitive, caring man. One who'd made her feel special and treasured in ways she'd only dreamed of before. It was an illusion, one that would pass once they put a stop to the sexual dance and satisfied their desires. Surely things between them would fizzle fast once the afterglow faded.

She was counting on it. Because she had to go home as planned and secure her father's future. But first she had to face Mac and all he had to offer. For a woman whose primary reason for being in Arizona was to attend a series of seminars on the benefits of risk management and investment portfolios, her nervousness now was ridiculous.

She forced herself out of bed and glanced in the mirror, pausing to brush her tangled hair. Then she drew on her reserve of courage and headed for the closed bathroom door. The worst thing he could do was throw her out, and what man in his right mind would toss a willing woman out of his bed or, in this case, his shower. Turning the handle, she walked inside.

A heavy beige curtain blocked her view. She didn't appreciate the obstruction until she realized it blocked his view as well. Silently, she stripped off her clothes, all the while pushing away every ounce of doubt that tried to creep in and stop her. Samantha Reed had always been a good girl. And good girls didn't seduce complete strangers.

Steam had filled the bathroom, accompanied by the fragrant scent she'd come to associate with Mac. The scent that wrapped itself around her heart and wouldn't let go. After she'd spent the past few nights cocooned in his arms, the smell was familiar and welcoming, giving her courage. Maybe Samantha Reed wouldn't seduce a man she'd just met, but *Sam* would. And Mac was no stranger, he was a part of her.

She paused only to brush her teeth quickly and grab a drink to ease her dry throat. "Would you mind some company?" she asked as she pushed aside the shower curtain a fraction of an inch and stuck her head inside.

She meant to meet his gaze. Instead, she focused on other parts of his anatomy and swallowed hard. Any adjective she chose would fall short, so she settled on magnificent…and large. Fully aroused and…

The sound of him clearing his throat grounded her thoughts. "I asked if you're here to watch or to play?"

She met his gaze. Amusement glittered in his eyes, but so did desire. Naked, unabashed desire. For her. At that moment, Sam realized she might have come seeking passion, but she'd also come looking for something far more important.

For once in her life, she wanted to be desired for herself. For the unique woman she'd become, not the obedient little girl she'd always been. Not for what services she could give to her company, or for how she could salvage her father's life, or worse for how lovely she'd look on her fiancé's arm, since she knew any beautiful woman would do. She wanted a man to need her, Samantha Josephine Reed, for the woman she was.

Mac did. He offered her that and more. Sam would always be eternally grateful for the gift.

Beads of water poured over his deeply tanned skin. Just watching him caused a quickening inside her. "I most definitely want to play," she answered.

"Thank God." She grinned, and Mac's heart squeezed tight in his chest.

He wasn't anybody's white knight, least of all Samantha's. He was a man, and right now he lacked the strength to say no. They'd been building to this moment from the second they met.

After pushing the shower curtain aside, he held out his hand. She slipped her fingers around his and stepped into the tub. All white and creamy skin, untouched by the sun's rays, broken only by darkened nipples and an even darker triangle of curls, she joined him. He let out a groan, thankful for her courage. He'd had his doubts this time would ever come.

He'd been wrong. Although he couldn't miss the signs of nervousness, the inability to meet his gaze and the slight tremor in the hand she placed in his, he sensed her certainty as well. She came toward him at the same time he gripped her waist and pulled her forward so she could join him under the warm, pelting water. He fused his lips to hers, her breasts, stomach and thighs melding with perfection against his already-rock-hard body. As satiny skin rubbed against him, her soft hands gripped his back and her mouth greedily worked at his.

She purred like a lost kitten having found its way home. The sexy little sounds and moans turned him on, and his erection pulsed against her stomach. Gripping her backside, he held her firmly against him, but her body glided over his, writhing and moving, seeking deeper, more intimate relief. He knew just how she felt. All he had to do was touch her and he *needed* so much more.

He figured there were two ways to go about this, short and quick or slow and deep. Damned if he wanted their first time to be fast and unmemorable, but if she kept up that squirming, that's just what it would be.

He glanced around the stark tub. His friend Bear wasn't into luxuries, and the shower offered none of the amenities Mac's did at The Resort. His gaze traveled upward. Except for a shower massage. A resourceful man, he'd make do.

Placing his hands on her shoulders, he looked into her eyes. Violet eyes glazed with passion stared back. "You came to play."

"Yes." The word came out a breathless shudder.

"I'm glad."

Her answering smile was nothing short of beautiful, but it contained all the pent-up anxiety she must have been feeling. Mac cursed himself for not dealing with it sooner. The minute she'd walked into the bar, he'd sensed the contradictions warring within her. She was a lady down to her dusty toes, which made the act to come all the more exciting and made his next move that much more important.

Soap and foam covered his hands. Instead of rinsing them off, he knelt at her feet and began lathering his way up her legs, her calves and knees. When he reached her thighs, she sucked in a deep breath and nearly lost her balance. "Brace your hands on my shoulders," he told her.

"I'm not so sure…"

"I am." He tilted his head backward. "Do you trust me?" he asked.

"Yes." She answered without hesitation.

"Then do it…so we can play."

She gripped his shoulders with her hands and he bent back to his task, working his soap-slicked hands up her thighs, toward the damp curls just waiting for his touch. There wasn't a sound except for muted music and water beating against the tub floor as he moved his hand and cupped her intimately.

"Oh, Mac." Her entire body shook in reaction.

He suppressed a shudder of his own. Tamping down on his desire in favor of hers, he slipped one finger inside her wet, warm heat. She moaned and dug her fingernails into his back. She jerked against his hand. The movement fed his desire, but he had other plans for Samantha.

He withdrew his finger, ignoring her disappointed cry and continued soaping up her skin. When he reached her rounded breasts, he nearly forgot his plan and lingered there for a while, fondling, holding and arousing them both. He dipped his head and captured one nipple in his mouth, tugging and pulling until she cried out his name and reached for his straining erection with her hands.

He grasped onto her wrists, halting her movement.

"Didn't your mother ever teach you to share?" she asked.

"She tried." He lifted her hair and nuzzled the damp skin behind her neck. "I wasn't any good at it. But I never minded taking turns, and this one's mine. Yours will come later."

Reaching behind him, he pulled the shower massage off the hook on the wall. "First we have to clean off all that soap."

A smile played around her lips. "I thought we were going to play." Her light tone told him she'd relaxed, which pleased him.

"Oh, we are." He grabbed hold of her leg and lifted it onto the side of the ceramic tub, then turned the jet spray to a light pulsing rhythm.

Her eyes opened wide.

"You said you trusted me."

"I do."

"Still?"

She nodded. "Considering you've been sleeping beside me without making a move...I think you've earned it."

She had no idea how damn difficult that had been. Another thing he loved about Samantha was her innocent lack of awareness. She had no idea how much she turned him on.

He focused the spray on her legs, rinsing off the

soap he'd spent so much time applying. "Back to the nice-guy thing again?" He didn't want to spook her. Keeping things light seemed the safest bet.

Angling his wrist, he directed the spray upward. Water sluiced down from the middle of her thigh, cleansing her skin. "You might want to hang on to me about now," he said.

She gripped his shoulders at the same moment he let the spray hit her intimately. Samantha whimpered, her body arching against the pulsing water jets. Her wanton response made him more determined to complete her pleasure.

He lowered them to the tub floor, settling her between the vee of his legs. Bracing her against his side, he nudged her legs apart and slipped his finger inside her, beginning a rhythmic sliding motion she picked up easily. Her body tightened and relaxed around his finger, which he eased in and out, pushing deeper with each successive thrust. Her jerking motions worked with him, while he used the other hand to let the shower massage pound against her swollen mound of flesh.

He wished he could see her face, but instead had to settle for the soft sighs and reflexive movement of her body rocking insistently against his. The constant friction of her back against his erection was almost more than he could stand. Damn, but he needed to be inside her, stretching her and filling her…. Without warning, she cried out her release, and the incredible sound triggered a climax of his own, one he hadn't expected and could not have imagined, not without actually being inside her.

With another cry, she collapsed against him. Mac dropped the handle and let the shower massage fling back until it hit the corner of the tub, its spray narrowly missing them both. He lay back, leaning his head against the wall. Water pounded around them, similar to the way his body still throbbed with aftershocks.

Samantha hadn't uttered a word. She hadn't looked him in the eye, either. He didn't blame her. How the hell had he taken such advantage without thought to her feelings? Because he'd stretched his patience and need beyond reason, Mac thought. Which was no excuse. "You're too quiet."

"Am I?" she murmured. "I was just thinking about a certain cliché. It's true, you know."

He wrapped his arms around her waist and buried his face in her damp hair. Feeling her soft body against his gave him more pleasure than any man should have. "What is?" he asked.

Her giggle vibrated against his chest. "Nice guys do finish last."

He tightened his grip on her and laughed, relieved at her response. Damn but he loved her. But he knew that wasn't something she wanted to hear.

WRAPPED IN A THICK TOWEL, still chilled from the remnants of a shower that had turned cold, Sam joined Mac in bed.

She forced herself to look at him, at this special man she'd allowed liberties she'd never imagined existed. "I just want you to know…" Embarrassed, she stopped. She felt the heat rise in her cheeks, but she had to continue. For all the time they'd spent together, they'd never actually discussed anything intimate.

"I want you to know I don't go around sleeping with…" She stopped again. Technically they hadn't slept together…yet. "Seducing…" Had she been the seducer or had he? She shook her head. "Showering with…" That was literally true, but the things he'd done transcended the definition of a shower. "I don't sleep around."

His hand cupped her chin, his dark eyes boring into hers. "Sweetheart, I never thought you did. In fact, if I had to guess, I'd say this was your first…shower." He grinned, and she couldn't help but smile back. Mac had such a disarming manner, his very presence relaxed her.

"I enjoyed it," she admitted.

Rolling over, he pinned her body to the bed with his. "I could tell."

"There's something else."

He propped himself on his hands, taking his weight off her chest. "Why am I not surprised?"

"I'm...safe. I just thought you'd want to know."

He raised an eyebrow. "So I don't need protection?"

"Yes. No. I mean, you do...need it. I'm safe in the medical sense." Her marital blood test had proved that fact. "But not in the pregnancy sense." Stupid, she knew. Though she'd come down here planning on sleeping with a sexy, sensual man, she'd also planned on making him use protection. So she'd be sure. She'd also planned on buying some herself, *after* she'd made her decision.

Then she'd fallen into a routine with Mac, one that came easily and without thought. She'd forgotten to worry about protection. She'd forgotten to worry about anything at all.

He grinned, obviously not the least bit put off or insulted by the topic of conversation. "You don't have to worry about me, either, except..."

"What?"

"I don't have any here."

"That's not a problem. Well it is, but..."

"We'll have to hit town."

She'd been wrong about something else, too. Their first time together hadn't made her want him any less. She sat up in bed, making a belated and unsuccessful grab at her towel. He laughed, and she was chagrined to discover that even his laugh aroused her. He coaxed her back against the pillows and ran a hand over her bare breast. "Slow down, sweetheart. We have time."

It was Sunday afternoon. Suddenly she felt like she was counting down instead of looking ahead to the rest of their week. *Stupid, Sammy Jo.* His finger drew lazy circles around her nipple. Without making contact, the pull went straight into her stomach, making her nipple contract and harden, begging for his touch.

She had less than four days to get this man out of her system so she could get on with her life. Alone.

"HEY, HONEY, ANOTHER round over here."

Sam eyed the men at the table in the corner. They'd been drinking steadily for the last couple of hours. She wondered how long they could keep it up. With each successive drink, their mouths became looser, their hands freer. As if they thought talking dirty and violating her personal space would turn her on. What it turned was her stomach. The last few nights had shown her these type of men weren't the norm around The Hungry Bear.

Forcing a smile, she glanced their way. "Coming right up." She dodged a wild hand and headed for the bar where Mac stood mixing drinks.

An emergency favor for Zee had dragged him out of bed almost immediately after the shower episode. She still blushed a deep red just thinking about it. He'd returned in time to open the bar. Sam had used the time to savor Arizona and attempt to convince herself she could walk away from Mac with her heart intact. She still didn't believe it.

She looked at him. He was wearing his standard faded jeans and a white T-shirt. An ordinary outfit, if Mac were an ordinary man. But he wasn't, as her rapidly beating heart could attest to. "Another five on tap for the corner table," she told him.

"They keep that up and I'll have to cut them off." He reached over and tucked a strand of hair behind her ear. The warm, thoughtful gesture caused a lump in her throat. "How're you holding up?" he asked.

"Never better. I've really grown to like this job. You meet all kinds of interesting people. And it's good exercise."

"I don't recall you needing exercise...." He leaned over the bar. She met him halfway, and his warm breath caressed her cheek. "And don't forget I've seen pretty much everything."

Her body heated up instantly. His seductive grin told her he'd accomplished his goal. He knew just how to arouse her.

"I stopped at the drugstore while I was out this afternoon," he whispered in her ear. The simple words set her aflame.

He straightened, continuing to work as if nothing unusual had passed between them. Only the unmistakable desire in his eyes and the clench of his jaw told her otherwise. He filled five glasses and began placing them on her tray. "I guess sitting behind a desk doesn't offer much in the way of exercise?" he asked, bringing her back to where they were.

"Not much. The walk to and from the train station does that."

He pushed her full order toward her. "A long walk must feel good after sitting behind a desk all day."

"Yes."

"You mentioned something about financial work, but you never said what…"

"I'd better go, the natives are getting restless." She deliberately cut him off. He'd never asked much about her life and she didn't want him to start now. If he crossed over the line, he'd go from temporary lover to…what? Someone she shared confidences with? Cared about?

She already did, which was why she had to keep some distance between them. At least her attempt at changing the subject appeared to work. He glanced toward her waiting customers and scowled.

"I wouldn't do that if I were you. It causes wrinkles, even in men." She ran a finger over the furrows between his eyebrows, until he caught her wrist in his hand.

"And I wouldn't do that unless you were looking to take a risk."

Little did he know she'd already taken one by being with him. "Such as?"

"You're avoiding personal questions between us, Samantha."

Not only handsome, but perceptive, too. Was there no end to his virtues? "Maybe, but anything more will only complicate things between us, don't you think?"

He studied her for what felt like an endless moment before he answered. "Things are already complicated," he muttered. "But you're right…the natives are getting restless." He grabbed a rag, turned away and began wiping down the bar where the foam from the beer had overflowed.

She longed to say something, anything to end the sudden chill. But what? *I'm a financial planner engaged to another man? I'm selling myself to the highest bidder? As much as I care about you, the course of my life is already set?* Somehow, she didn't think he'd appreciate hearing any of those answers any more than she liked thinking them.

She lifted the tray and walked away. Mac watched her hasty retreat, admired the movement of her hips and wished like hell they hadn't been interrupted earlier.

"If you ask me, I'd say you struck out," Zee said with a chuckle.

"No, just crossed over the line." An imaginary one Samantha had drawn ever since their conversation about her father. Anytime he'd asked, she'd been unwilling to reveal any more about herself. With their week running out, perhaps she thought it best to keep her distance. Perhaps it was time to enlighten her that the end of the week didn't have to mean *the end*. He shook his head.

"If you want the lady to confide in you," Zee said, "seems to me you ought to do the same."

Mac agreed, but Samantha wasn't ready. What had begun as an innocent deception now loomed large between them. She was emotionally skittish, and he had no desire to give her additional reason to run. Whatever was keeping her from him, he didn't want his secret to make things worse.

His gaze fell on her as she worked. Ironically, as she clammed up emotionally, she opened up sexually. Who'd have thought she would greet him in the shower? Having sampled only a part of what he wanted from Samantha, Mac wasn't dumb enough to think he could keep his hands to himself any longer. Once he closed for the night, nothing would stop him from having Samantha in his bed. Hot and eager, warm and wet, pulsing around him...

"Easy, boy." Zee's voice shattered Mac's daydream.

The older man had followed his line of vision and caught him drooling over Samantha. He hadn't been privy to Mac's thoughts, but the way the codger's mind worked, he'd probably come too close to the erotic truth for Mac's peace of mind.

"She's pretty good at this," Zee said.

Making her way around the table of men, Samantha placed a beer in front of each customer, ducking, chiding and putting them off with a laugh or a shake of her head. Mac had to give her credit. She'd learned quickly how to handle a table of eager men.... Except for the guy she served last.

His hand lingered on her waist despite her vehement disapproval, and when she tried to take a step backward, she was stopped by a firm palm on her behind and a whisper in her ear. On the rare occasion when Mac had seen it happen to Theresa, he'd always handled the situation with a detached calm that resulted in a quick resolution. No one got their feelings hurt or their bones broken. Something changed inside him when the woman being pawed was Samantha.

A raw possessiveness flooded his veins, but he forced himself to give her a second to handle things before he went charging in. He gave her a second too long, he realized as the guy rose to face her and placed a hand on her breast. Mac rounded the bar and headed for Samantha quicker than Zee could spit.

Apparently she'd learned more than Mac thought. She was also faster, because by the time he reached the table, the guy was wearing his beer on his jeans.

"Put a leash and a muzzle on your customers, Mac." She glared at the offender who was busy wiping down his wet jeans.

"Zee…" Mac nodded in the drunken guy's direction.

The older man understood. He grabbed the patron, who began ranting about harassment, and led him and his friends to the door. He'd make sure they knew they'd worn out their welcome and check that someone sober drove home. Bear's father might act outrageously at times, but when called for, he could be a formidable opponent and a good friend.

Once Mac was sure they had gone, he turned his attention to what was important. He reached for her hand and wasn't comforted to find her fingers trembling inside his. "Samantha…"

She shook her head, cutting off anything he might have said. "I'm fine." But her pallor told him otherwise. "You should have heard the things he said. He was crude and acting… I don't know, entitled. Like because I'd served him drinks, I'd like to cater to him in other ways, too." She kept wiping her hands on her clothes, as if she could wipe away the memories as easily. "Just because I serve drinks for a living doesn't mean I'll…*service* any slimeball that walks in here."

She spat the last few words with such anger, Mac didn't think now was the time to remind her she… Hell, he didn't exactly know *what* she did for a living, but he knew it involved high finance and not serving drinks in a backwater bar. But she respected those who did, which made his respect for her inch up another notch.

He glanced at his watch. Closing time was still forty-five minutes away. "Okay, folks. Whatever you drank last, consider it last call." Because the incident had been loud and public, the grumbling remained at a minimum.

Clouded eyes met his. "You don't have to close early for me. I told you I'm fine."

He wasn't. He reached for her, his hand grazing her cheek before he pushed a strand of hair off her too-pale face. "I'm closing," he said with finality. "If not for you, then for me."

"But Bear…"

"Left me in charge. I figure that gives me some rights around here."

"Who am I to argue with the boss?" she asked, some color coming back to her cheeks.

He braced his hands on either side of her face. "You did a great job taking care of yourself tonight. But I want you to know I wouldn't have let him hurt you."

"I know. Like I said, he didn't. He just…violated me somehow."

A lady like Samantha, from the world *Mac thought* she came from, wouldn't be used to harsh words from a drunken idiot. "Give me a few minutes to close up and this will all be a distant memory." He'd make sure of it.

Zee returned. "You okay, honey?"

She turned her sunny smile on the older man. "Fine. And thanks for everything."

"My boy doesn't run a trashy joint. I'm sorry…"

Waving away his apology, she grasped his gnarled hand. "I know what kind of place this is, Zee. And you don't have to apologize for it. Either of you." Her gaze took in Mac, as well.

Mac the bartender. Suddenly his deception didn't sit well with him. In fact, it turned his stomach.

Zee turned to Mac. "I'll get going and let you take care of things here." The old man shot Mac a pointed look before heading for the door. "Oh…" He turned back. "You still planning on taking that drive to Sedona to see your mama tomorrow?" he asked Mac.

"No. I'll put it off a few days." No sense visiting his sister and mother with a woman in tow. Mac didn't have the answers to the questions his family would surely ask.

"Okay, let me know. Maybe I'll tag along with you when you go," Zee said.

Mac smiled. "They'd like that."

"Maybe Sammy Jo would like to join us," Zee whispered as he took his leave.

Mac rolled his eyes, then wrapped his arm around Samantha's shoulders. She curled her body against his, and he took comfort in her being near.

He swallowed a raw curse. Because when sexual desire took a back seat to concern and other emotions he'd never felt before, Mac knew he was in trouble.

CHAPTER SIX

THE SMALL APARTMENT had an even smaller balcony that overlooked the main road. Sam hadn't noticed when she'd first arrived because she'd had other things on her mind—like thanking God she still wasn't stranded in the desert—nor had she become aware of it afterward, because a sexy man had stolen her breath away. But now that she'd discovered the sanctuary, she made it a point to take refuge there now.

Sitting on a folding lounge chair, she curled her legs up and took in the view of the dark road lit only by a full moon and the occasional headlights of a departing vehicle. One by one, the last of the cars pulled out of the graveled parking lot below. Soon not even the roar of an engine intruded on her solitude. A cool breeze wafted on the night air, much the way contentment floated through her veins. Not even tonight's incident marred the sense of peace she'd found.

Peace she shouldn't be feeling. Not when she was lying to a man she'd grown to respect, dodging honest questions because she was afraid that if she let him get to know her, she'd want to know more about him, too. How would she leave then? How would she walk out on a life and a man she feared suited her far better than the ones she'd be returning to all too soon?

Choices, she thought. Life came down to choices, and she'd made hers the day she put Tom's ring on her finger. It wasn't important that worry over her father's future had prompted her decision, or that she'd promised her dying mother. She'd accepted. Given her word. Which made her time with Mac temporary. She'd just live their fantasy to its fullest before slipping away too soon. Her heart thudded in silent but furious protest.

The slam of the door jarred the otherwise silent night. She had company. When he joined her outside, he filled the small area with his presence. Big, solid, comforting. That was Mac. If he was in a room, she knew it. Seconds later, comforting turned to wanting. A smile touched her lips for the first time in more than an hour and she welcomed the change.

Everything Mac made her feel was good. Without waiting for an invitation, he swung one leg around and fit himself behind her back, drawing her into his arms.

Why fight it, Sam thought, nestling into his embrace. "I overreacted tonight," she murmured.

"Tossing the beer in his lap? Nah, he deserved it."

"Not that." Next time she'd try for a pitcher instead of a glass. "Getting so emotional."

"Somebody grabs you after you say no, I'd say you have a right to any damn emotion you please."

"I guess. I knew I had nothing to worry about. We were in a public place." And she'd known Mac was standing guard, and she trusted him to be there if she needed him.

"A bar is a different atmosphere than what I'm used to. In the workplace, the episode downstairs would have been sexual harassment." His hands flattened on her belly and she relaxed against him. Warmth traveled from his body to hers in a never-ending current that sensitized her skin and caused a delicious pulse to hammer in her veins.

"Are you saying that guy didn't sexually harass you tonight?" He lifted her shirt and stroked her stomach as he spoke.

"No, just that I wasn't prepared and I should have been." She'd removed her bra when she'd changed into the oversize T-shirt she was wearing, and now his thumbs softly grazed the bottom of her breasts in a rhythmic lulling motion.

She sighed and tried to focus on their conversation, although it was hard to do when his roughened fingertips stroked her already-charged skin. "But a stranger whispering what he thought were erotic things in my ear, and putting his hands on my body…" She trailed off because even as she spoke, the realization sunk in.

What would her marriage bed be but a place where a stranger pawed her, groped her…. *His* hands on her stomach, not Mac's. Hopefully he'd leave out the titillating whisperings in her ear, she thought as she shivered with dread and disgust. Oh, God, how could she have agreed to the marriage? How could she go through with it now, having known Mac? She felt her stomach muscles quiver and tremble.

Without warning, his fingertips, along with the blissful gliding motion, stilled. "What's wrong?" She tipped her head back so she could see his face, and immediately understood what she read in his eyes.

Turning so she could face him, she ended up straddling his legs and placing her knees on the outside of his thighs. Of course, that meant his groin nestled between her legs, full, warm and inviting, but she couldn't concern herself with that now, either. The heated throbbing wouldn't be ignored, but she tried because his feelings meant more to her than sexual need. *Uh-oh*.

She forced herself to deal with what was important and looked at Mac. "Whatever you're thinking, stop it now."

"Even if it's true?"

She met his gaze. Clear, slate-colored eyes stared back. "It isn't." This man had ceased being a stranger the moment he'd caught her in his arms.

A connection existed between them, one she didn't understand and couldn't explain. If she was certain of nothing else, she knew he felt it, too. "If you'd stop worrying that I'll fall apart like some china doll, you'd know it, too." She placed her hand on his chest. "Listen to your instincts. Are they telling you we're strangers?"

"They're telling me I want you." A mild way of putting it, Mac thought. *Need* might be an even better word.

"No, that's your body talking." She laughed a husky, sexy sound that turned him on even more. Considering his erection pulsed between the vee of her legs, he figured she was right.

She was right about something else, too. No way in hell was he a stranger whispering erotic things in her ear. But what was he to Samantha? He had no idea. She never said. In fact, she'd made it clear she never would.

Since he was keeping secrets of his own, he hadn't wanted to pressure her. He'd hoped in time she would confide in him of her own free will, but that day seemed far off. He'd gotten involved in the first place because he sensed there was something special about Samantha. He had omitted a few details because he desired her respect. Now that he had it, parting was the last thing he intended to do.

"So have we resolved that dilemma?" she asked, easing herself more fully on top of him.

He exhaled a harsh groan as her warm body, covered only by thin lace, settled over his groin. Was it his imagination or had her seductive grin, an upward turn of her lips, gotten bolder as their time together wore on?

He grabbed her neck and brought her head within inches of his own. Her soft scent enveloped him, cushioning him in a cocoon of desire. "One dilemma down, one more to go," he said, before covering her lips with his.

He tasted her, first with his tongue, then with his whole mouth, until not only did she kiss him back, but she gave as good as she got. She devoured him and all he could do was feel—her pliant mouth moving against his, her hands plowing through his hair and the urgent thrusts of her hips as she tried to get closer.

She bucked against him, searching for fulfillment until he felt himself grow and swell against her damp heat. When she'd correctly decided that wouldn't work, she sat up, which pressed her concealed flesh tighter against him, and reached for the hem of her T-shirt.

Too soon, too fast, he thought. Much more and there wouldn't be time for everything else he wanted to do to her, with her. "Sam…" His belated grab for the shirt came too late. She'd pulled it off and tossed it aside before he even had a chance to stop her.

"Sweet heaven," he muttered. Faced with her bare body covered only by a scrap of underwear, those rounded breasts and her "come hither" expression, he didn't give a damn that she'd flung her T-shirt over the balcony rail.

He bracketed her hips in his palms and looked up at her. Violet eyes glazed with passion stared into his.

"I can't hold off any longer."

Her eyes darkened even further. "Did I ask you to?"

Mac took her words as an invitation. Easing the bit of lace down her legs, he was rewarded when she caught her breath in anticipation. Desire warred with gratitude for his good fortune. Someday he'd have to thank whoever rented her that clunker of a car, but right now, he couldn't think of anything but Samantha.

Juggling their position, he sat upright against the lounge, forcing her to move and balance on her knees before him.

"Listen, Mac..." Even the way she said his name turned him on. "I think I was too...forward, that's it, too forward." She gestured over the balcony to where she'd tossed her shirt. "I never should have done that..."

"Did anyone ever tell you that you ramble when you're nervous?" He grinned, realizing the intimacy of the position she'd maneuvered had finally gotten to her.

Those contradictions not only intrigued him, they aroused him. Even her rosy blush made him hard. He wanted this woman and the innocent joy she brought to his life with a fierceness he'd never known.

"No. That is, I'm only nervous when I'm..." Her hands gestured to her beautifully naked body. "I mean I'm only nervous...when I'm with you...like this." She tried to cover herself with her hands. "So I think..."

His fingers *slipped* from her hips to her thighs. She gasped aloud. "Don't think, Sammy Jo." Her eyelids opened wide. "And definitely don't move." He parted her legs with his hands, dipped his head and tasted her warm, waiting flesh.

If he died and went straight to hell in the next moment, he wouldn't give a damn, Mac thought. Because he'd just been as close to heaven as a mortal could get.

HER KNEES BUCKLED and her body swayed. Not exactly the reaction Sam had envisioned having, but oh, sweet heaven... And that's where he was bringing her...now that he'd switched their positions and lowered her onto the lounge chair. In her wildest fantasy—and since meeting Mac she'd had plenty—Sam had never dreamed it could be like this.

The skin on her thighs tingled, chafed from where his whiskers had rubbed her flesh. Her muscles quivered, seeking more of the exquisite sensations.

"Don't ever shave that mustache," she murmured. "At least not while I'm around." A little voice reminded her that wouldn't be much longer. She ruthlessly pushed it aside.

"Wouldn't think of it, sweetheart," he chuckled. And then his mouth worked its way up her inner thigh, purposefully letting his mustache trail against her skin once more. At least she thought it was on purpose, because the rasp of male whiskers had her body jerking upward, nearly taking her off the seat.

"Easy, sweetheart." He spoke in a husky voice, then let his tongue soothe the chafed surface on her thighs.

"Easy for you to…" Her words ended abruptly as he lowered his head and his mouth covered her *there*. Again. She shut her eyes and fell backward on the chair. She hadn't known what she was setting herself up for or how incredible it would feel, but Mac was teaching her. Apparently, her body learned quickly.

Waves of pleasure coursed over her each time his agile tongue darted in and out of her pulsing flesh. Need curled in her muscles and her stomach contracted. His mustache worked in erotic conjunction with his mouth and she arched her back, silently reaching higher, searching for more, asking for…

"Mac?"

He met her gaze, and the desire she read in his eyes shook her to the core. Then he shocked her again by placing his palm over the juncture of her thighs and rocking gently with the heel of his hand. She moaned at the assault, trembling as the incredible pressure inside her continued and was startled to realize he watched her the entire time. Though she should have been embarrassed, his gaze turned her on.

With each upward thrust of his hand, with each jerk of her hips, his eyes darkened even more. Pleasure rolled through her. She wanted to wait, she wanted him inside her, she wanted…to scream…and she did, as she tumbled over the peak of the most spectacular climax she'd ever had. The subsequent waves pulsed and pounded through her body long after she'd crested and fallen.

At some point she must have closed her eyes. When she opened them again, he stood by the chair and scooped her into his arms. "Where are we going?" she asked.

"Inside. You woke most of the wildlife and I wasn't even inside you. Can't risk you rousing the nearest neighbors."

She grinned, the smile of a satisfied woman, she knew. "How far off are they?"

"Well over a mile." He lay her down in the center of the double bed. His eyes twinkled with mischief. "But I have faith in you."

BEFORE SHE COULD REPLY, he began stripping off his clothes, rendering Sam speechless, which considering her case of nerves was saying a lot. What was about to happen… Well, it was the real thing.

She told herself to grow up. After all, this wasn't her first time. But it was with Mac, a little voice in her head warned. And you've given him so much of yourself, what's left? that persistent voice asked. She pushed the thought aside, and when he joined her on the bed, she welcomed him with open arms. Because he would be giving her everything she needed from this week.

And more, that voice said. This time, Sam didn't just ignore the voice, she smothered it by burying herself in his strong arms and solid body. He rolled her onto her back and straddled her, catching her hands above her head with one hand.

As she stared into his dark eyes, desire struck her again. Hard. His breathing was labored, as if he'd been the one who'd just… She shook her head to dislodge the memory of having his hands on her body, his eyes watching her as she came. But the image stayed and she couldn't help wondering, Was such continuous passion between two people rare?

Not if the chemistry was right, she told herself. And that's what she and Mac shared. Chemistry, that's all. She realized she was telling herself an awful lot of things tonight. She hoped they weren't lies—she had no choice but to believe them.

Not if she wanted to remain whole. Remain the same Samantha who'd walked into this bar a few days ago. *Good luck, sweetheart.* Oh, Lord. That was Mac's voice she heard in her head.

His lips nuzzled the side of her neck and she sighed. His hands slipped to the juncture of her thighs and she knew he found her wet and wanting. She lifted her hips as he eased one finger inside her. A soft moan escaped her lips and another finger joined the first.

"I'd like to take my time," he groaned, arousing her with penetrating thrusts. "To wait."

Her head fell back against the pillow. "Why?"

He chuckled, a relaxed sound that eased her mind. "Because I want you to remember this." As if realizing he'd just reminded them the end was coming, his laughter ceased.

Her chest constricted at the same time warning bells sounded in her brain. Ignore them, she insisted. Only this time, it wasn't so easy. But dwelling on the inevitable wouldn't serve any purpose.

Leaning forward, she eased one hand out of his grip and grasped him in her fingers, running her hand down the length of his erection and back again to the tip. A small drop of liquid coated her palm.

This time she couldn't control her thoughts. Life, love, babies. Mac's life, his love, his babies. All possible, but not for her. If this were another time, another place, she'd forget caution, forget being sensible and go with her feelings. But her emotions had to remain locked away. If she didn't acknowledge them, then they didn't exist.

Right? No little voice answered. Right? Silence. Oh, she had a bad feeling about this.

His groan echoed in the small room, bringing her back to the present. "Mac?"

Sweat beaded on his forehead. "Sorry, sweetheart, but waiting won't work."

"I don't recall asking you to wait." She smiled and let him retake her hand and lock it back with the other one above her head. "But you do have to trust me if you want to reach for that box over there."

He grinned. "You won't touch?"

"Not unless it's necessary."

He released her hands to grab for protection. She immediately plucked the foil packet from his fingers, feeling little embarrassment. With each successive moment of intimacy, Sam felt less inhibited. She could be herself with him, something that had never occurred before…and never would again.

"You promised not to touch." His lips twitched in amusement.

She shook her head. "I said I'd touch only if necessary. And it is." Because if she didn't touch him, she might die and then she'd never experience having him inside her. So he had no choice but to forgive her for taking liberties with her promises. Just as she had no choice but to forgive herself for *feeling* when that hadn't been part of the plan.

She covered his erection with one languid stroke,

making sure her hands grazed and lingered longer than strictly *necessary,* purposefully playful and light. But as he raised himself over her, Sam realized she wasn't playing anymore.

She lifted her pelvis at the same time he grabbed her hips in his hands and joined their bodies with a smooth, easy thrust. Then he let out a groan, a deep, masculine grunt of satisfaction that coiled her stomach into an even tighter knot. He stilled, letting her body stretch to accommodate him. The gesture was thoughtful, but unfortunately for Sam, unnecessary. Her body accepted him like a lost part of itself had come home at last. Every muscle inside her felt him pulsing and alive, filling her. Completing her.

Oh, sweet heaven, she was in more trouble than she thought. Her eyes grew damp. Was that a tear trickling down her cheek? Oh, no. No, no, no, no.

"Sam?"

She forced her eyelids open and plastered a phony smile on her face. "Yes?"

His thumb caught an errant tear and he raised his finger to his mouth for a taste. "Salty," he said. "I hurt you."

"Oh, no." That much she could say honestly. She lifted her hips, drawing him in deeper, groaning at the penetration and perfection she'd found. "How could that hurt me?" How could anything this man did ever hurt her?

"Oh, baby, it can't." Then he surged into her completely, losing himself in her.

Fully impaled on his strong erection, she decided since she'd come this far, she might as well enjoy the rest of the trip. But as she began to move, to grind her hips against him and recapture the waves of delight she'd felt earlier, she realized this was much more than a vacation gone right. This was beyond fun and games, beyond sex.

She'd lost the ability to hold a part of herself back and found herself giving it to Mac instead. As he pumped himself into her, each time harder than the last, her body rose to meet his. The sighs, the moans, the gentle coaxing, they came from her lips but also from her heart…because her emotions swamped her, forcing her to let go, to give without reservation.

Her body felt full to bursting, when without warning he slowed the pace. "Don't stop," she whispered. If he kept moving and she kept feeling, she wouldn't be able to think. And Sam wanted to remain lost in Mac with no intrusions.

"In a second. First I need this." His hands roved over her breasts, cupping and caressing her already-hardened nipples, drawing them into tight distended peaks.

"Oh, Mac. Please…"

"I will. Just as soon as I do one more thing." He pulled her upward, so she felt every hard ridge of his arousal, stopping so she was poised at the tip of his erection.

"What?"

Bending his head, he opened his mouth over her breast and sucked on her tender nipple. He nibbled, tasted and soothed, all the while rocking her swollen body against his rigid muscle. Waves didn't wash over her, they pummeled at her and demanded release. "Oh, my…" She choked on her words just as he lunged into her again.

As he surged inside her, seeming to grow larger and pulse stronger with each thrust, Sam didn't need long. He'd pushed her close to the edge already and she didn't have far to go. So when he stiffened and groaned her name, his final plunge pushed her into the ultimate oblivion she so desperately sought.

Her breathing came in labored gasps and her body trembled as she opened her eyes to find the world still waiting for her. The world she wanted but couldn't have…with the man who still remained inside her. The man she didn't just have sex with, but had made love to instead.

"You are so incredibly…beautiful."

In her soul, she knew he meant more than surface beauty and she tucked the knowledge away in a private space in her heart. But he had to stop before things became too serious between them. Before she did something stupid. Like fall in love with him.

She forced a laugh. "I bet you say that to all your women afterward."

He raised an eyebrow in blatant disbelief. "Right," he muttered. "And every woman I've ever been with is thinking about the others while I'm still inside them."

She cringed as a wounded expression flashed briefly across his face. She'd meant to protect herself, instead she'd hurt him. He started to withdraw from her when she realized she couldn't let him go. Not like this.

"Mac, wait." She curled her fingers into his back, stopping him. "I'm sorry. Please… Forget what I just said. Put it behind us, let's just pick up where we…" She glanced down. Their bodies were still joined and she felt him within her. Heat and desire swamped her again, along with a whole host of emotions she refused to name. "Oh, I don't know what I'm saying, except don't leave me."

"You're rambling," he said, and grinned. His cocky smile put her at ease. At least he wasn't angry. If she could put aside her emotions, they could, in fact, pick up where they'd left off. She felt the beginnings of a smile of her own.

"Rambling's a good sign," he said, his fingertips tracing her lips. Her tongue darted out to taste his salty skin. She watched as his eyes clouded even more.

"Why's that?" she asked.

"Because according to you, you're only nervous when you're with me…like this. So I'll excuse that reference to other women."

Part of her was relieved he was so willing to drop the subject, while another part wished he'd reassure her that there were no other women…none that counted, anyway. But she had no right to want what she couldn't offer herself.

"Relax, sweetheart. I won't hold it against you." As if to prove it, he paused for a long, hard, meaningful kiss. His tongue licked her lips, then probed at her mouth until she let him inside.

When he came up for air, Sam was gasping herself. "I'll be right back, and then we *can* pick up where we left off."

With Mac gone, Sam curled into a tight ball, wrapping the blanket around her. Then, despite the warnings her heart was giving her, she rolled against him when he came back to bed and cuddled into his warmth.

"Thank you," she murmured.

"For?"

"For not being angry, for being there…for being you."

He brushed a kiss over her lips. "I could say the same. You are something special, you know."

"No, I'm…"

"Yes, you are," he said firmly. "I've never known anyone like you."

"Mac, don't. You don't realize what you're…"

"You're right, I don't. You jump each time I get close, and I'm not talking about sex." He let out a frustrated groan. "But this time…" She placed her finger over his lips.

Her heart warred with her mind. She wanted to let him finish, to hear what he had to say and enjoy the closeness they were beginning to find. But that would be selfish because why let him in emotionally when she still had to walk away in the end? If the choice were hers, she'd stay in this bed forever.

The thought sent her plummeting back into reality. Hers wasn't the only life at stake. Her father's well-being and recovery hung in the balance. She needed his bills paid, his mind clear and his way of life assured. Marrying Tom was the only solution…even if she loved Mac. *Oh, God.*

Unable to cope with that, she thought of him instead. To let him in now would only hurt him later, and he deserved so much better than that. Pushing him away was the only form of honesty she could give, so she reached between them and grasped him in her hand, surprised to find him hard and aroused again. "You said something about 'this time'?" Her voice came out a husky purr.

Desire filled his eyes, but so did dismay. "I know what you're doing."

So did she. Distracting his emotions by turning

him on. She wasn't playing fair, but in her heart, she was protecting him. She forced a smile. "I should hope so."

"Sam…"

She silenced him by stroking his flesh until he groaned and rolled her on top of him. His erection pulsed against her, making her wet, making her need him inside her.

She met his dark gaze. "I want you again."

He grinned. "Don't sound so surprised."

She'd meant to distract him and succeeded in arousing them both instead. She'd accomplished her goal, but instead of feeling good, she was aching inside for all that she wanted and all that could never be.

Not wanting to think anymore, she rubbed herself against him, coaxing him to do exactly as he suggested earlier. Sam lost herself with the man she loved, but couldn't claim as her own.

CHAPTER SEVEN

MAC WOKE WITH THE SUN, which meant he'd had little sleep the night before. Not that he was complaining. The naked woman now curled beside his equally naked body made a little lost sleep worthwhile. He stretched and rolled away from her gently. The sunshine beckoned. After pulling on his jeans, he went downstairs and walked outside, but the warmth he found there wasn't the same. Mac didn't care. The great outdoors offered him what he needed most.

Wide-open space and lots of it.

He sat on the wooden porch outside Dear's bar and stared at the empty stretch of road before him. Could a woman complete a man? Mac hadn't thought so, at least not before he'd met Samantha. But once his body had been held tight inside hers, with her wet, moist heat contracting around him, he'd revised his opinion. Not that he'd had the foggiest notion what to do about it except enjoy the moment, but he'd looked into her worried gaze and realized that the moment had passed. He'd have preferred to see passion or contentment filling her beautiful eyes. Instead she'd been troubled.

And then she'd spoken. Other women? He laughed aloud, the harsh sound echoing around him. Since meeting Samantha, he hadn't given other women a passing thought. Since making love to her, and that's exactly what he'd done, he didn't want to. But she sure as hell made it a point to remind him that he should.

He ought to feel slighted and was worried when he didn't. Because he understood Samantha. She wasn't like other women he knew, which was what drew him to her in the first place. Figures. The first time he meets a woman who lacks pretense, who doesn't want anything from him, who likes the man he is and not the money he has, and she obviously wants nothing to do with him beyond...

Wednesday. Just a few more days.

Damn.

Understanding her the way he did, he knew the barriers she erected made her feel safe, so she raised them whenever he threatened her "other" world, which he seemed to do with increasing frequency. But that was only fair since she threatened not only his world but his sanity. Until now, he'd not only let her get away with it, he'd raised a few barriers of his own because she had never indicated she wanted more than what they shared now.

Mac didn't kid himself. He'd sensed something

unique from the start, but he'd allowed himself to enter a purely sexual relationship, hoping to build more. He had, and together they'd progressed beyond anything either of them had envisioned. For the first time in his life, he was ready to deal with those implications. Most women would swoon at his feet in exchange for a ring. They would be pushing for undying declarations of love while convincing him to fly them to Vegas for marriage.

Thanks to his misguided bragging in his youth and the number of repeat female clientele, most women knew more about Mac than they should. Not his Samantha. At this point Mac had no problem telling her, either. But she wouldn't let him in.

Instead of trying to draw out his emotions, she hid behind sex. Which, he reminded himself, wasn't necessarily a bad thing. Most men would enjoy continuous and varied lovemaking with Samantha. Lord knows Mac did, just not when the lady in question was avoiding him in other ways.

He placed his hands behind his head and leaned back. From his reclining position, he could see the bottom of the balcony, and the memory of Samantha flinging her shirt over the rail replayed itself in his mind. He pushed himself to his feet, but he already knew he hadn't stumbled across the garment this morning.

"What kind of wildlife would be interested in a shirt?" he wondered aloud.

"You looking for this, boy?" Zee's laughter broke through the early morning air.

"I should have known." Mac snatched the cream-colored top out of the old man's grasp. "Don't you ever sleep?"

"Nah. Especially when I figured you could use a hand cleaning up after last night. How is she, anyway?"

He glanced up at the closed window and tried not to picture Samantha as he'd last seen her, naked, one bare leg and an even more enticing bare cheek sticking out from beneath the covers. "Still sleeping."

"Wore her out, did you?"

"Not now, Zee."

The older man followed Mac up the wooden porch and leaned against the corral-style railing. "So you finally fell in love. How's it feel?"

"Like hell," Mac muttered, grateful to have a friendly ear.

"Welcome to the world, boy." Zee grinned. "Just don't tell Bear. Once he gets his woman, I want some grandbabies to bounce on my lap. But yours would be equally as good, so tell the lady the truth and live happily ever after."

"I can't get her to relax enough to tell her my first name," Mac muttered.

Zee shrugged, then placed a gnarled hand on Mac's shoulder, a gesture he'd done so often through the years. "Maybe you haven't tried hard enough. If you want something, go after it. If you don't, you really don't want it that bad."

Mac mulled over that piece of advice while he tossed her shirt into the bar and rejoined Zee on the porch.

"You clean up from last night?" the older man asked.

"Not yet."

"Well, get outta here. I got Hardy and Earl coming by. They've got nothing to do, anyway, and they'll be more than happy to help."

"I can't let you do my work for me."

"You don't, and I'll tell Bear you're leaving ladies' lingerie all over the damn bar. If I had a sexy woman waiting for me, I wouldn't be down here soaking up sunshine. I'd be upstairs soaking up something else." The old man choked on laughter at his own joke.

"Okay, but I owe you one."

"Introduce me to the next lady you meet at The R—"

"So tell me, where's he picking up women, Zee."

At the sound of Samantha's sexy voice, Mac turned. She stood in the doorway, hugging the frame.

"Well, hello, Sammy Jo." After his greeting the older man grew silent. Unusually silent. For the first time, Mac witnessed Zee at a loss for words and realized the older man was protecting his secret.

"Details," Samantha said. A spark settled in her eyes that Mac strove to comprehend. "I want to know where and when." One part determination, he decided, the other part jealousy. He hoped.

"About what?" Zee asked.

It wasn't like Zee to play dumb, and Mac felt bad putting the old man in the middle. "He wants me to introduce him to the first good-looking lady I meet on our trip today," Mac answered for him.

"Trip?" She swung herself out the door, excitement tingeing her voice, a renewed bounce to her step. The yellow tank-top dress she wore clung to her curves in a way that had him drooling. It'd be a long day watching her without touching, but that was exactly what he planned to do.

Once again, for both their sakes, he had no choice.

"Where are we going?" she asked.

"Someplace relaxing, where we can get away from the bar and you can enjoy the weather." He knew just where to take her. Sometime after Zee made his offer, Mac decided Samantha needed space from the intensity they'd shared.

She was on vacation and needed to feel like it, not to mention the fact that he could use a breather himself.

SAM HADN'T REALIZED how much she needed to get away for a while until Mac suggested they do just that. She'd woken up alone, and a whole host of insecurities had greeted her. They came back to haunt her now. So what if it had been good for her? Maybe it had been lousy for him. She bit down on her lower lip, recalling the times and ways they'd made love. Three condoms' worth plus some other imaginative maneuvers. Who'd have thought they came in packages of a dozen? Mac, that's who. No, it had definitely been good for him, too.

But maybe he'd had enough. That was possible. How many men wanted to wake up with a woman once they'd…consummated their relationship, let alone spend another few days with them? Perhaps this trip was more about getting away so he wouldn't have to…

She shook her head to dislodge that horrible prospect. "What do I need to bring?" she asked.

"Yourself."

She glanced at his serious expression. No sexual innuendo danced in his eyes or sounded in his voice. In that moment she knew something had changed between them. "Okay." Her throat grew suddenly dry. "When are we leaving? After we clean up the bar? Because I started while you were outside talking to Zee, and I got as far as—"

"Zee's taking care of things around here today."

Zee was awfully quiet, too, she realized. No banter, no jokes from either man. Why did she feel like she'd walked into an episode of *The Twilight Zone.*

"Okay, what's wrong?" she asked the two men.

"Not a thing. Just too much partying yesterday," Mac said. This time his eyes met hers, and hot passion shimmered in their depths. Last night hovered between them. Warm bodies, hot sex, a release and a sharing she'd never forget.

Apparently he hadn't put it behind him, either. Which meant whatever was bothering him had nothing to do with regret. She hadn't realized how much she feared his turning away from her until she thought he had.

Relief swamped her, and she let out the breath she hadn't been aware she was holding. Blood began to flow back to her fingertips because she'd unclenched her tight fists. She shouldn't be bouncing off his emotions, but she was. And until she heard how he felt, she wouldn't be truly at ease.

Zee cleared his throat. "You go get yourself ready. Me, Earl and Hardy'll finish up around here." The older man gestured to the pickup truck bouncing into The Hungry Bear parking lot.

"Are you sure we shouldn't stick around and help out? We could get started a little later on."

"Positive. Zee and I have an agreement. Anyway, let 'em earn their keep," Mac said with a grin. He gestured inside the bar and she turned, assuming he'd follow.

She took two steps and trod on the shirt she hadn't noticed in her earlier haste to meet up with him outside. She scooped it into her hands.

"Can't have you making a habit of leaving your clothes around this bar, Sammy Jo." His warm breath caressed her ear, and the teasing note had returned to his voice.

"No, we can't," she agreed. She turned around, grasping the shirt in her hand and wringing it like a wet towel. "Listen, Mac. If you're feeling obligated, like you have to shuttle me around until I leave, don't. I can take care of myself and find plenty to do. I can even check into the hotel a couple of days early...assuming there's a room, and if not I can find a motel..." His firm hand clapped gently over her still-moving mouth. She tasted warm, salty skin.

"Everything is fine. You hear me? Fine. And you're not leaving for that conference until the last possible minute."

Relief made her overstressed muscles turn to mush. "It's just that you..." *Spit it out, Sammy Jo.* There was little-enough truth between them, on her part, anyway. She didn't need to hedge now. "It's just that you seemed so distant when I got out here, so I thought...well you know what I thought."

He removed his hand from her mouth and braced his palms on her shoulders. "I didn't know how you'd be reacting to the morning after, so I was giving you space."

"What if I don't want any?" There would be plenty of distance between her and Mac soon enough, she thought, trying to swallow the painful lump in her throat.

"Then I won't give you any." He dipped his head for a leisurely kiss, warm enough, wet enough, special enough to reassure her. "Now, are you ready to head a little farther west?" He eased the shirt, which now looked like a wrinkled rag, out of her hands.

She stared into the dark depths of his eyes and smiled. "Yes." Anything he suggested sounded good to her. "I don't know what you had planned, but when I was straightening out back by the storage room, I found an old picnic basket. I could throw in a few of the things we picked up at the store and we could eat on the road."

"You sure you'd like that better than a restaurant?"

"Hmm. Wide-open spaces versus a crowded room. Hordes of people rather than just you and me? Come to think of it, a restaurant sounds much better."

He laughed and took her hand. "Come on. Let's pull some things together before we're eating under the midday sun."

Sam followed him inside to pack and get ready, determined to make the most of their time. Time that was already ticking away much too fast.

AFTER FINDING A SPOT beneath a tree, Mac unloaded their packages while Samantha spread a large blanket across the grass. A warm breeze floated on the dry air. Turkey sandwiches, chips and cola went down quietly, the silence telling him she had finally relaxed. In the ensuing stillness of the desert, Mac enjoyed something that until now had been foreign to him. Comfortable silence with a woman by his side. He hadn't realized such a phenomenon could exist for him.

She bit into her chips with gusto and crunched loud enough to wake the wildlife, then glanced at him and shrugged. "What can I tell you? They crunch when you munch."

He burst out laughing. Damn but she made him feel good. Crumbs had fallen over her yellow top and he reached over to help her clean up. His hand brushed her breasts, and her nipples turned to rigid peaks.

She sucked in a startled breath and he shrugged. "Sorry."

"No you're not."

He grinned. "You're right, I'm not." He reached into the basket for another cola. "Drink?"

She rolled her eyes. "No, thank you. But it is hot." Despite the wide leaves overhead, the Arizona sun beat down on them, and she plopped a wide-brimmed straw hat she'd bought in Cave Cove onto her head.

Resting her chin on her knees, she looked into the

sky and sighed. "Who said you don't see heaven on earth?"

He eased himself closer. "I guess you like it here?"

"What's not to like?" She lay down on her back, letting the hat fall behind her head, and stared up at the sky. Wanting to see her perspective, he joined her. Their arms aligned and touched. Neither pulled away.

"It's enough to make me want to consider a geographical change," she murmured.

"Seriously?"

"No." She answered quickly. "But a person can dream, can't they?"

"Nothing wrong with that." As long as he could convince her to make those dreams a reality. To do that he had to understand what made her so skittish.

"So where are we, exactly?" she asked.

"A deserted stretch of land." Mackenzie land, but Mac didn't think she was ready to hear his secrets just yet. "It goes for miles in either direction."

Squinting into the bright glare of the sun, she shaded her eyes with her hands. "And that large hotel in the distance?" She rolled onto her side for a better view.

"A place called The Resort."

"You're kidding."

"No, why?"

Her shoulders rose and fell. "It's where I'll be going for my conference," she murmured in a voice he had to strain to hear. A voice that told him how much she disliked the prospect.

That pleased him. The location of her conference was another story. The jig was up. Mac had never been into absentee management, and she'd know within an hour of check-in that he owned the place.

He pondered the unexpected news in silence, deciding how to use her conference location to his advantage. At the very least, now he could set the stage and tell her in his own setting, on his own terms. Once he'd thought things through, he couldn't believe his luck.

When she walked out of The Hungry Bear, she wouldn't be leaving him after all. As owner, he had access to all the guest registration cards. He knew exactly where to find her, and he had no intention of letting her get away.

"The conference you mentioned. It's at The Resort?"

"Yes." She settled herself more comfortably on the heavy woven blanket and eased herself backward, until she snuggled into him.

Her small backside wedged against his stomach and groin. He swallowed a groan, suppressing desire in favor of the information he wanted her to reveal. He had a number of business conferences scheduled for later in the week and he tried to recount the possibilities.

"Let me guess," he said. "You're an insurance salesman."

Her throaty laugh rumbled against his chest. "Funny, Mac. You already know I'm a financial planner. I'm attending workshops on financial gain and risk management."

"I knew there was a brain in that gorgeous head. So are you meeting clients or superiors there?"

"Both. The mornings and afternoons are filled with seminars that'll help me make wiser and safer investments for my clients. Then I'll take some clients to lunch, and my…boss will take me and some of the firm's larger clients to dinner."

He smoothed her long strands of hair out of his face, then rested his chin on her shoulder. "So tell me. When you were a little girl, did you dream of being a financial planner?"

She laughed at the deliberate absurdity of the question. "I dreamed of being a ballerina, then when I turned out to be uncoordinated, I dreamed of being married. Love, a fairy-tale wedding and happily ever after."

"And the financial thing?"

"Came about when I realized a savvy woman doesn't rely on a man to support her. And because my college grades showed I had an uncanny ability with numbers. I invested some money my father had put in my name when I was young. I made a nice, tidy sum. Turns out I was good at taking risks, too."

He grinned, thinking how much they had in common. He'd taken a risk investing all the family money in turning the small bed-and-breakfast into a first-class resort and spa. He could have lost everything.

Samantha's biggest risk seemed to be letting herself get close to him. He glanced over. At least she'd begun to open up. Now that he knew he could surprise her at The Resort and tell her everything there, he'd bought himself more time.

His gut told him he had her heart, but he had yet to win her trust.

"So tell me. What are your dreams, Mac?"

"I didn't think you wanted to know."

"I've shared mine, so fair is fair. Besides, what are dreams but fantasies, and we've already shared those."

Had they ever. Just the memory made him hard. He wanted to be inside her again, but the timing was wrong. If he broke off their conversation now, he'd lose Samantha for good. "Okay."

He'd never shared his dreams with anyone before and found it hard to know where to begin. When he'd sold off acres of his father's land to expand the hotel, he'd also kept in mind a promise he'd made. "I'd like to build a house on a wide-open stretch of land," he told her. This land.

"I can see why."

His father had wanted surplus acres kept in the family for future generations of Mackenzies. Mac had complied with that request, and though his sister still owned her land, she couldn't live there now. As for Mac, there'd been no reason to build a house for one person, and lately he'd begun doubting he'd contribute to the continuation of the Mackenzie name. Then a bedraggled female had stumbled into a bar and given him cause to rethink his future.

"A large house?" she asked.

At least she was interested. "As big as you want," he said.

"Mmm. Ranch-style," she murmured obviously getting into the fantasy. "Children?"

"One or two." With black hair and violet eyes.

"Two. No, make that three. Being an only child is lonely. Two boys and maybe a girl running through a real home decorated in beige, white and cocoa brown."

"My favorite colors," he said, glad she couldn't see his grin.

"Stylish," she continued. "But comfortable enough to live in without feeling stifled. Like you'll break something if you let loose and feel free."

"Is that the kind of place you grew up in?" he asked.

She stiffened. As if his question shattered the fantasy and reminded her she'd gone too far. "I…"

His hand stroked up and down her arm. "Keep going," he whispered.

"I…I grew up in a beautiful home, but the house was full of things meant to be viewed, not touched. My mother loved fine things, my father loved indulging her."

She laughed, but the sound was strained. "Let me rephrase that. He loved her. Period. There wasn't much room left for me."

His grip on her arm tightened, as if he could reassure her with a touch, or infuse her with the love she'd been lacking up until now. "I'm sure your parents loved you," he said. How could they not?

"Of course they did. But it was just leftover affection, like whatever they could spare when they weren't together."

He thought about his sister and the fun, the laughter and pranks they'd played on each other. He recalled his parents' frustration with their children, but he also recalled their love. Love that included their kids as well as each other.

"Their loss." He didn't know what else to say, but he intended to make sure she never felt as lonely and vulnerable again.

"I know that…now."

"And you really want three kids?" he asked

lightly, beginning a rhythmic lulling motion of his hand, encouraging her to answer.

"Yes." She rolled and he expected her to move away. Instead, she turned so she was facing him and brought her body flush against his. Her hands rose to cup his cheeks. "Do we have to talk anymore?" she asked.

He'd pushed her far enough. If he'd needed a sign that she wasn't ready to hear his secret, she'd just provided it. She'd given him enough for one day.

"No. There's too many other things we can do."

"I like the sound of that," she murmured.

He locked their hands together and brought her fingers to his lips, kissing the ring he'd bought that first day. Such a simple ring for people with such complicated lives, he thought. But it was that simple twisted band that made Samantha happy.

He pondered the irony of finding a woman content with sentiment instead of show and wondered how she'd react when he told her he could afford much more than the small ring that had captured her heart.

He'd tell her. After the rest of the week had passed and once he was back on his own turf. A woman who desired the fundamental things in life would surely understand why he'd omitted mentioning his wealth before getting to know her first.

One thing he knew for certain. She cared more for him than anything he could buy her.

Rolling onto his back, he brought her with him,

so her body fit tight against his. His erection settled between her thighs.

"Ever make love in the great outdoors?" Her eyes glittered in the afternoon sun.

He laughed. "Does a balcony count?"

She shook her head. "Afraid not."

"Then the answer is no."

"I could rectify that." She shifted so his erection sat poised for entry, the only barrier between them their clothes.

Her sensual moan shook his common sense, but he managed to swallow a groan of assent. She smelled like his Samantha, a scent that aroused him beyond reason. Her hands shook in his and he knew she felt the same. Her body, hot and wanting, ground against him. For a woman filled with embarrassment in the beginning, she'd grown comfortable around him fast.

His gut told him this maneuver was meant to dodge emotional intimacy. His body, near to bursting, asked him who the hell cared. From somewhere, and he had to dig pretty damn deep, he found a remnant of self-control. "It's tempting, but I have to say no."

"Because we don't have protection? There are other ways to enjoy ourselves."

Because no matter how much he wanted her, he refused to let her hide her feelings and emotions behind sex. Again. "There's something I'd rather do," he told her.

She raised an eyebrow in eager expectation. "And that is?"

"Hold you." With a jerk of his hips, he dislodged her from her perch and rolled so he could capture her in his arms again. She squealed her displeasure, but he ignored her protest. Grasping her slender hips, he pulled her against him, her back solid against his erection.

"At least I know you want me," she whispered.

"Wanting isn't the issue."

"What is?"

"Being with you in the time we have left."

Silence greeted him. Well, what had he expected? An undying declaration of love? An admission that she didn't want to leave? The honesty they'd shared today had been enough of a start.

The sun beat overhead. A breeze that grew warmer by the hour blew around them, and a bird chirped in the distance. Bit by bit, her tense muscles slackened and relaxed.

"You make me happy, Mac." Easing herself onto her back but not out of his reach, she grasped his hand and held on tight.

The truth from her heart. As a gift, he'd accept it. He reached over and tucked a strand of hair behind her ears. "I try."

She smiled and he raised her hand to his lips, kissing each of her knuckles in turn and then the ring that would bind them forever. Whether she knew it or not.

CHAPTER EIGHT

TWO DAYS HAD PASSED since he had held her in his arms so tenderly. Other guys would have jumped at the chance for easy sex, but not Mac. The man she loved. Damn him, anyway. Why did he have to be so chivalrous? So irresistible? So very hard to walk away from.

The last forty-eight hours had been spent in an almost unbearable combination of dialogue and cuddling. No sex. After he'd rejected her advances, she knew better than to try again. And he hadn't, either. The white knight she'd met that first night had reasserted himself. And she loved him for it.

Sam hustled between the tables, serving customers and taking orders, but even the loud crowd at the bar couldn't take her mind off the war raging inside her. What did she owe her father? More important, what did she owe herself?

Although Mac had never mentioned a future, he had forced her to take a long, hard look at the woman named Samantha Josephine Reed. What she discovered amazed her. She'd never known she was capable of intense passion, the kind that meant tossing aside her inhibitions and letting go. With Mac, she could be wild, wanton and not the least bit embarrassed.

Okay, maybe a little embarrassed, she thought, remembering the red marks she'd left on his shoulders and the shriek that echoed throughout the Arizona countryside. But he really did do amazing things to her body with that mustache. Just the thought had her clenching her thighs together with need. She shook her head to dislodge the memory before she spilled the drafts of beer on her tray.

He'd also taught her the meaning of love. Soul-deep, touch-your-heart, burning love. The type she'd believed existed only in fairy tales. The kind a woman was lucky to experience once in a lifetime, and even luckier if she was able to keep it.

Well, Sam had found it. Not that she had any idea whether Mac's feelings echoed her own. He certainly acted the part of a man in love, but that was the point. How much was real, how much fantasy?

Though he'd encouraged her to open up to him, every time she thought she caught a glimpse into his heart, he retreated. Because she'd intentionally pushed him in that direction? Or because he too had wanted to leave reality behind for a short time?

A time that was almost over. Sam had to walk out

of this bar tomorrow, hopefully with more dignity than she'd had walking in.

She served a small table of customers by the front door and ducked outside for a breather. She inhaled deeply. Now that she wasn't an underdressed hiker, the cool night air was but one thing she'd grown to love about this place.

"Hey, Sammy Jo." Mac's voice broke the stillness of the night and interrupted her thoughts.

A good thing, considering the direction they were taking. Good heavens, was she even considering breaking her engagement? Who would believe good, well-behaved, sensible Samantha Reed would do such a thing? Well she'd never believed herself capable of seducing a stranger, either, but that's exactly what she'd done.

She'd gone and fallen in love with him, too. Old-fashioned, head-over-heels, happily-ever-after in love. But did she have the nerve to act on her feelings when it meant going back on her word to Tom, breaking her promise to her dying mother and most important, betraying the father who was counting on her? Could she risk losing what sense of family she'd managed to find? In essence, turning her back on every honorable ethic that had been instilled in her since birth?

But where were her father's ethics when he'd allowed her to accept a marriage proposal that bordered on extortion, a little voice asked. Since meeting Mac, she'd done a lot of unique things, and talking to herself ranked right up there. It seemed to be becoming a habit, she thought. An annoying one, especially when that voice seemed to make more and more sense.

"What are you doing out here by yourself?" Mac asked.

"Taking a break. Waitresses get a couple a night, don't they?"

He swung himself onto the wooden porch railing. "Mine do."

"Who's watching the bar?"

"Who do you think?"

She grinned.

"What else are you doing out here?" he asked.

"Mmm. Just thinking." Her gaze traveled over the body she'd already memorized inch by tantalizing inch. "Any reason you wear the same type of clothes to work each night?" she asked.

He glanced down. Not that he'd notice, but the white shirt pulled tightly across his chest, and his faded jeans stretched snugly over his muscular thighs. Tailor-made for his athletic build.

He shrugged. "Cuts down on that shopping men hate so much."

She laughed.

"And?" he asked.

"And what?"

"And what else is going through that beautiful head of yours? You only come outside for air when you need time to think."

She cursed his perception. She loved how well he knew her. But she hadn't come to any conclusions herself yet, and she certainly couldn't share the process with him. "I was wondering how to tell Zee."

"Tell Zee what, honey?" The screen door opened wide and the older man stepped through.

"Now it's a damn convention out here," Mac muttered.

She glanced from Mac to the older man, both people she'd grown to care about. "How to…" She cleared her throat. "How to say goodbye."

Mac frowned at her choice of topics. Turning to Zee, he asked, "Who's watching the bar?"

Zee didn't answer. Maybe because his mind, too, was on her departure. A light wind picked up and Sam shook her hair out of her eyes. She twisted the ring on her finger without meeting Mac's gaze.

"You ever think of giving people privacy, Zee?"

"If Sammy Jo wants me gone, she'll say so."

Mac rolled his eyes.

She didn't think she'd ever meet a character like Zee again. Despite his antics, the old man had a sharp wit and an even sharper mind. She had a hunch that Mac relied on Zee's aged wisdom more than he let on. She loved the old coot for that, Sam thought. At least when she was gone, she'd know someone was looking out for her sexy bartender.

A lump formed in her throat, and she reached out to pat Zee's weathered hand.

He turned to Mac. "You ever think maybe I want to say a personal goodbye to Sammy Jo? Besides, you have thirsty people inside, so get."

Sam looked into Mac's serious gaze and her heart twisted. Both knew they had all night ahead of them. And neither wanted to think about tomorrow.

"You heard the man, Mac." She forced a smile. "Now get."

"I've got the two of you ganging up on me," he muttered as he rose and headed inside. The door slammed behind him.

"He's a good boy, Sammy Jo."

"I know."

"And you're a fine lady. I knew it the minute you hobbled into the bar. Don't ask me how. At my age, if I can't trust my instincts, I got nothing left to trust."

"You're perceptive," she agreed.

"But you're both young. And stupid. You think because you are young you've got all the time in the world." He looked up into the star-filled night sky and shrugged. "Maybe you do, maybe you don't. But if you ask me, it'd be a damn shame to waste any of it."

"Life's more complicated than that, Zee."

He placed his hand over hers. "Only if you make it that way, honey. We've all got choices. You make the right one."

She sighed, wishing the right thing for herself didn't involve so much grief and heartache for others. "Whatever happens, I'm glad I met you," she told the older man.

He smiled. "Me, too. Bear called and he'll be back tomorrow, his lady in tow. Think I'll be called Grandpa any time soon?"

She grinned. "I hope so."

"Think you'll stick around long enough to meet my son?"

"What I think is that you're trying to work your way back to the subject of what I'm planning to do."

His cackle echoed into the night. "You're pretty perceptive yourself. At least I know Mac found himself a woman who won't let him get away with any crap."

She most certainly wouldn't, Sam thought. And immediately wondered when she'd decided that.

MAC SAT ON THE EDGE of the bed and stretched his arms over his head, groaning in what had to be absolute exhaustion.

"Long night?" Sam asked. She glanced out of the bathroom where she'd been washing up to see him flop backward, hitting the mattress hard.

Good. He wouldn't be joining her any time soon.

If he peeked inside, she'd lose her nerve. Another glance told her he'd kicked his feet out in front of him.

"You have to ask?"

"No." She understood only too well. An emotionally draining week lay behind her. Every night at the bar had been physically exhausting, and tonight was no different. But she refused to let a week of passion-filled bliss end on a down note.

Tonight was their last time together, and no matter how chivalrous he thought he was being, she intended to get under his skin one final time. They deserved closure. She *needed* to feel him inside her one final time. With a little luck, she'd give him something to remember, too.

"The bar was busy tonight," she called out to him. "More than usual?"

"About the same. Bear won't complain that I lost business while he was away."

"Good. Have you rented above this place long?"

She thought she heard a grunt, but with the water running from the faucet in the sink, she couldn't be sure. "Can't hear you," she called. "But I'll be out in a few minutes."

"Take your time."

She paused to splash cold water on her face and brush her teeth before undressing and redressing, making sure the hooks and clasps latched onto their proper mates. The whole process should have taken no more than a minute, but she'd never worn a contraption like this before and her shaking hands added to the ordeal.

"The darn thing should have come with an instruction manual," she muttered. She didn't know how she'd walk out of the bathroom dressed like this, and she wanted desperately to change into the nightshirt lying in the other room. Instead she snapped the last clasp in place and drew a deep breath. She'd bought the lingerie on a whim, brought it with her on impulse, but never, ever had she planned on facing a live male while wearing it.

That was before she met Mac. He'd changed her plans. She feared he would change her life. Right now she needed to make sure *he* was occupied and not peeking.

"Listen to us discussing the day's business," she called out. "We sound like an old married couple."

Silence punctuated her statement. Silence that gave her time to think and realize she'd blundered. "Oops. I probably shouldn't be joking about being married with a man I've known less than a week." More silence. "The M-word probably has you thinking of ropes, as in a noose around your neck. Ball and chain, maybe." She laughed aloud, a nervous laugh, and not only because he still hadn't answered. She'd just described her views on her upcoming marriage, the thought of which frightened her more every minute she spent with Mac.

Speaking of whom, maybe he'd fallen asleep. No, she couldn't get that lucky. "Okay, Mac. I get the point." She drew a breath for courage and prayed he wouldn't think she looked like a fool if he was up.

Considering the prolonged silence, she doubted he was awake, which didn't stop her from rambling, but did give her the courage to walk into the room. "I know marriage wasn't the brightest thing to mention to you, considering you're just my..." She stopped cold at the sight that greeted her.

He lay on top of the covers, wearing nothing but a pair of skimpy briefs and his amused but always sexy smile. He'd crossed his arms behind his head. "I'm your what, sweetheart?"

Mac nearly choked when Samantha walked in. She was clad in a black lace one-piece getup, with a push-up bra exposing her breasts, a meshlike design covering, or rather uncovering, her midsection, and sexy lace underwear connected by crisscrossed straps to thin garters, which drove him wild. "My God, that thing cannot be for real."

Wrong thing to say. She darted for the bathroom so fast he had to belly flop across the bed in order to reach her before she slammed the door in his face.

He managed to grab her wrist, though she tried to duck inside the other room. "You had the guts to put it on, so don't run out on me now."

"I don't know what I was thinking," she muttered. "I look stupid."

He raised an eyebrow in disbelief. He realized the nerve it must have taken her to put the outfit on, but he still couldn't believe she could look at herself in a mirror and not know. "There are a lot of words I'd pick to describe how you look, Sam. *Stupid* isn't one of them."

"Really?" she asked in a soft voice. "Like what?"

Releasing his hold on her, he backed up and sat down on the edge of the bed. "You come out of that bathroom and I'll tell you."

She moved to the entrance, and Mac took that as his cue. He leaned back on his elbows and studied her. She stood in the door frame, black lace silhouetted by the white molding. Long legs, silken skin and hidden secrets all his to explore and unravel. He swallowed hard. "You look…sexy, for one thing."

She took two hesitant steps forward on bare feet. Her toenails were painted a glossy red. Funny, but he hadn't noticed before now.

"What else?" she asked.

"Hot," he said in a seductive whisper. "Red hot."

Her hesitancy seemed to vanish as she tossed her mane of black hair over one shoulder and took three more steps toward him. Close, but not close enough.

The pulse worked in her neck, teasing him, tempting him to taste, if she let him near.

"Wild," he continued. "Wanton..." Her violet eyes were wide with wonder as each word brought her another step closer. "Seductive, desirable..." He held out a hand. "Erotic, sensual..." She laced her fingers through his, and he pulled her so she landed on top of him on the bed. "And mine."

Her luscious scent enveloped him the same way her long limbs wrapped themselves around him. He pushed his hands into her hair, winding the strands around his fingers and tugging her head toward him so he could seal his words with a long, mind-drugging kiss.

His lips parted, her tongue took advantage and Mac groaned, crushing her to him with his arms. With Samantha, he didn't have to coax a response. Their rhythms met and matched, slow and surreal one minute, hot and devouring the next.

When she lifted her head, she was panting as hard as he was. He managed to hang on to reality by a slender thread. "You never answered my question," he said.

"I don't remember any question." By the dazed look in her eyes, he believed her.

"I'm your what?"

Her cheeks turned a fiery red. "I thought you were sleeping."

He grinned. "No such luck." He slid his hand over her waist, feeling the combination of warm lace and cool skin. Deciding he liked the feel of her skin best, he settled his hand on her behind. "I'm your... what?" he prompted again.

"Lover," she muttered without meeting his gaze.

His gut constricted. He'd sensed her intention all along, but he disliked hearing it stated so baldly. He had every intention of changing her mind, after he calmed her fears and reminded her of how perfect they were together. He'd spent the last two days cementing the emotional bond between them...as much as possible given her tendency to withdraw. But he wasn't about to pass up one last chance to be with Samantha. In this bar, in this place where she'd come to belong.

"I am that," he told her. And he planned to be much more.

He let his other hand travel over her hip until he was able to edge one finger beneath the lace border of the lingerie she wore. Her breath hitched and he grinned. "You always travel with this in your suitcase?"

"I saw it in a store and..." She blushed again. "I was curious."

"About?"

"What it would be like to wear it. Whether I'd really feel hot, sexy...any of those words you used before. I never actually planned to wear it for a man."

He felt absurdly pleased by her answer, because she'd changed her mind and had dressed in sexy lingerie, just for him. Another part of her answer bothered him, though.

"Are you telling me you never felt any of those things before?" He touched her intimately, finding her slick and wet. She moaned softly in his ear. "Because you're so damn responsive, I'd find it hard to believe."

"Oh, Mac." Were those tears glistening in her eyes? "Would you believe me if I said I only felt those things, felt that way, with you?"

"And that's a bad thing?" He licked the errant drop of moisture on her cheek with his tongue.

"No, it just is," she murmured.

He hated seeing her upset. "Now that you've had the experience, what do you say we get you out of this contraption?"

His question had the desired effect and her mood shifted. She grinned. "I'd like to see you try."

Rolling off him, she wriggled to the top of the bed, giving him an enticing backside view. He groaned and followed her up to the headboard. A small white tag hanging from behind her neck caught his eye.

He grasped the label and caught a glimpse before she turned to face him. "Hmm. Expensive little number."

"What?"

He chuckled. "You left the price tag on."

She buried her face in her hands. "I'm mortified," she cried. "I can't even perform a seduction right."

"Trust me, sweetheart. You seduced me just fine. There's only one problem."

She raised a questioning brow.

"You spent a lot of money on something I'm going to rip off you sometime in the next few seconds."

"Oh, really." Not to be outdone, she reached over and cupped his groin, running her hands up and down his full, straining length. "If you ask me, it was worth every penny," she purred.

He stilled her movement with an iron grip. "Not if you keep that up." He clenched his teeth in an effort to stop the waves of need that threatened to erupt too soon.

Her soft laughter only inflamed his desire.

"Witch," he said, and she grinned. "You are something, Sammy Jo." This woman in his arms did things to his heart, body and soul. She was an enticing combination, his innocent seductress. No schemes, no guile. Just Samantha.

"Oh, yeah? Then prove it."

"Fatal error," he growled, and reached for the spaghetti strap on her shoulder.

Beneath the sexual innuendo, the flirtation and the seduction lay deep emotion. Sam knew it. She'd bet Mac did, too. The thought didn't scare her as much as it should have considering how much still lay in their way.

The elastic straps held her arms prisoner against

her side. Not that she couldn't move if she wanted to, but considering the hungry, possessive look in his eyes, why would she want to?

Charcoal eyes bore into hers. "Never dare a man on the edge."

She grinned. "Is that what you are?"

With one finger, he traced the scalloped lace covering her cleavage. "I don't know, sweetheart. You tell me."

She dared a look downward. His erection seemed to bulge and grow larger beneath her heated stare. "I'd have to say you're right." Her tongue darted out, moistening her dry lips.

He exhaled a low growl. "Do that again."

She licked her lips, and Mac ran his finger over the moisture she'd created. He tasted salty and male, and just touching his skin with her tongue caused a tight pulling sensation between her legs.

"And all this self-control is costing me a lot, wouldn't you say?" he asked.

"I…yes."

He placed his wet finger over the mesh covering her nipple. She moaned. He rubbed back and forth, increasing the friction until a rigid peak formed under his touch. As if there were a string connecting her breasts to the damp heat between her legs, she felt the tugging stretch and expand and she clenched her thighs together to ease the strain.

"Not that I mind, but at least one of us ought to take advantage, wouldn't you agree?"

At this point, she'd agree to anything he said or did. He seemed to sense how quickly he'd brought her to the edge and yanked the lace cup down, revealing her to his sight, exposing her for his mouth. His hand began a rhythmic kneading motion of her breast at the same time he clamped his lips over her rigid nipple. She caught a glimpse of his dark hair against her white skin and felt the coarse strands against her flesh.

This was right. She knew in that instant, she belonged to him. The knowledge freed her mind in a way she hadn't allowed all week. He nipped with his teeth and soothed with his tongue until she couldn't stand the unfulfilling pressure. She needed him inside her, completing her, but the pulsing, pounding wouldn't be denied.

Grabbing his wrist, she shoved his hand between her legs. He gave one upward thrust with the palm of his hand against her swollen heat. That's all it took and Sam climaxed, a huge wave washing over her, causing her to shake with unrestrained passion and need. Though he'd taken the edge off her desire, she still felt swollen and empty. Needy because she'd come without him inside her.

"You know that self-control I mentioned earlier?" he asked in a hoarse voice.

She forced her eyelids open. "Yes."

His slate eyes appeared black. "It's gone, Sammy Jo."

With what Sam thought were extremely nimble fingers under the circumstances, Mac freed the clasps on both her shoulders and the garters. He tore the garment off her with much more ease than she'd put it on. She would have been annoyed, if she didn't want so badly to be naked beneath him.

His briefs went flying. He put on protection faster than she'd thought possible, and finally she felt his weight on top of her. Flesh to flesh, he was warm, strong and solid, everything she'd ever wanted and never had the courage to dream of.

His arms bracketed her head. "Look at me."

Not a difficult request, Sam thought. She focused on his face, the dark, deep-set eyes, the intense stare, high cheekbones and firm lips she'd grown to love.

"And remember," he muttered. Without warning, his hands lifted her hips and he thrust deep, penetrating her with one hard push.

She gasped in surprise, then trembled when emotion took over. He hadn't filled her with himself, he'd become a part of her. She didn't know when it had happened, nor did she care. Lifting her hips, she accepted him completely, her gaze never leaving his as his body fused with hers, deeper than she'd thought possible.

So this was love. It was something beyond knowledge, something you experienced and felt in combination or not at all. She moistened her lips and moved her mouth over his, slowly, erotically, so she knew he tasted her.

His harsh groan filled her ears. When his mustache scraped her skin, she moaned, bucking against him.

"Sweetheart, you're killing me. I wish I could wait, but I…" He exhaled a groan. "I can't."

"Then don't," she murmured against his lips.

He moved inside her, once slowly and then with quick penetrating thrusts neither could control. Sam felt each one in her heart, as if by joining bodies, their hearts and souls had connected as well. She'd needed him so badly, and apparently he'd felt the same. He climaxed at once and she tumbled right after him, falling headlong into waves of sensation and pleasure.

THEY LAY IN SILENCE. Only the sound of the rain hitting the pitched roof broke the comfortable stillness that hovered between them. "I didn't know it was going to rain," she murmured. She tucked her head against the curve of his arm and shoulder.

"It's been known to happen." Inanities seemed appropriate about now, Mac thought. After what they'd just shared, words would fall short. They lapsed back into a quiet understanding.

"What's your full name?" she asked softly.

Her words took him by surprise. He'd have thought she'd rather retreat than move forward. But he preferred her curiosity to any sort of backslide.

He played with the ends of her hair, brushing them against her cheek. "It's Ryan. Ryan Mackenzie."

"I'd never have guessed. And who called you Mac?"

He shrugged. "My mother liked the name Ryan. My father called me Mac. No rhyme nor reason. It just was."

He felt her smile against his arm. "I like them both," she murmured.

Not about to let an advantage slip by, he said, "Your turn, Sammy Jo."

She sighed. "Samantha Josephine...Reed."

"The first two are a mouthful, hmm?"

"Yes. But they're refined and classy, or so my parents thought. Image is important in my family. Which is why my father's problems seem so insurmountable to him." She cleared her throat. "Anyway, they called me Samantha, and as a result, so does everyone else."

"Except me."

She laughed. "Except you."

If image was so important to her family and friends, his perceived background, his bartender job, might be what was bothering her. He didn't for a minute believe *she* didn't accept him for who he was. Who she thought he was, he reminded himself. But she might know she'd have a difficult time explaining their relationship to her father and her friends.

She had nothing left to prove to him. He loved her and believed she loved him. He ought to just let her off the hook. "Look, Sam."

She eased herself on top of him. "We have an hour or so left till sunrise. Do you really want to spend it talking?" she asked.

Her warm body spoke to his. Renewed desire surged through him. "As difficult as it is to say, yes."

"But I don't. I need this time together." She pushed his hair off his temple and touched her forehead to his. "Without pressure, without...anything but us." She brushed a kiss over his cheek and then on his lips. "I need you, Ryan."

He groaned. He could have resisted anything but his first name coming from those lips. He reached for another condom on the nightstand. By his count, that made four.

If she wanted to wait, he'd wait. He knew where to find her.

CHAPTER NINE

MAC FINALLY FELL ASLEEP near dawn, and Sam crept out onto the balcony to watch the sun rise over the distant mountains. Even the incredible beauty, the deep hues of yellow and burnished red glowing against the increasingly blue sky, couldn't hold her interest. Her gaze kept straying back to the man inside.

He'd wanted to talk. She'd brushed him aside. She'd had no other choice. She had a life waiting. She and Mac had shared a week. An incredible, amazing, never-to-be-forgotten week. Could it be more? She didn't know because she hadn't let him finish. She couldn't, not until she'd sorted out her personal problems.

Thanks to Mac, she felt ready. He'd taught her how to find the woman inside herself. A woman she hadn't known existed.

She'd spent her life searching for something that had been forever out of reach. She'd done so by pleasing first her parents, then Tom. Never had she put her own needs first. She hadn't even thought to try. Without realizing it, she'd allowed herself to become empty and unfulfilled. When her mother had asked for her promise, Samantha thought she'd found their acceptance at last. She was wrong. She'd had it all along. She just needed more than they were capable of giving.

But she was no longer a little girl seeking affection. By the time her father had brought himself to the brink of disaster, bailing him out had been second nature. Sacrificing herself was something everyone expected. Even she hadn't truly questioned her decision. Until Mac had shown her all she'd be giving up.

In return for all he'd taught her, she'd given him the only gift she could before leaving. She'd asked him his name and offered hers in return. Freely given information without him having to push.

But she owed Mr. Ryan Mackenzie so much more than she could ever repay. And not just for giving her the passion-filled week she'd sought, or the love she hadn't. She gripped the iron railing in her hands as she faced the truth. She owed him for making her face herself.

And having done that, she knew.

She could not marry Tom.

If she turned her back on the woman she'd discovered, she would betray her innermost self. Worse, she'd betray Mac and their time together. Sam would never do that. She couldn't. She respected him too much to throw away everything he'd given her, not the least of which was a renewed sense of self-worth. She'd learned she couldn't sell herself for anyone, including her father.

What about your father, a little voice in her head asked? How could she bring herself to betray him? *You aren't responsible for your father, Sam.* Mac's words came back to her and she knew he was right. Her father was the parent, she was the child, and very often those roles became reversed with age. But that didn't mean she had to sacrifice everything. *"You can't give up the rest of your life because he's having trouble with his."* Mac was right about that, too. There had to be another way. *"Be there for him, advise him and help him if you can."* Together, she and her father would work through this, and she'd be there for him every step of the way. He'd be stronger for the experience, just as she'd be stronger once she told both Tom and her father the wedding was off.

Her stomach contracted, tightening into a knot as she acknowledged what awaited her. An annoyed and humiliated fiancé, a betrayed parent and the unemployment line. Because once she ended her engagement, Sam had no doubt Tom, in his position as her boss, would terminate her immediately. And then?

Tom would move on, find another trophy to dangle on his arm and a competent financial planner to replace her. As for her father, she'd talk to his doctors and figure out whether he was capable of working again. Relocating seemed like a possibility for them both and would spare him Tom's wrath and the loss of status and dignity. One thing she knew. Her only parent would forgive. She had to believe that. After all, her mother and father had adored one another. Didn't she deserve the same? She'd agreed to this marriage because of a promise to her mother. A promise that had given her the sense of belonging she'd desired from parents who had loved, but hadn't known how to give in the ways a child needed.

But she was a woman now. One who'd been shown all she wanted out of life. She would never love anyone the way she loved Mac, and if he didn't want her forever, she'd rather be alone than settle for less. To do otherwise would demean them both. As she walked away from the balcony and back into the room, she laced her fingers over her stomach, trying without success to still the churning inside.

Why did doing the right thing have to hurt so much? Though she planned on coming back, she didn't know what awaited her upon her return. In silence, she packed her bag and paused by the bed one last time. She glanced down at the man sprawled on top of the covers and tried to swallow the lump in her throat.

She hated to leave him this way. She hated to leave him any way, but she had no choice. Too many unresolved issues remained in her life. If she stayed, she'd be tempted to throw herself into his arms, declare her undying love and refuse to face the outside world. If she stayed, she'd have to listen.

A part of her didn't want to hear him say he'd wanted their fantasy week and nothing more, though she knew she might have to face that eventually. But there was the other possibility. That he'd want her forever. Her heart beat more rapidly at the mere thought.

Sam wouldn't know what Mac desired until she confronted him. And until she freed herself from the engagement that bound her, she had no right to ask.

Leaning down, she brushed one last kiss over his lips. "I love you," she whispered softly.

Rolling over, he threw one arm above his head, but he didn't stir. Would he understand or would he hate her for slipping away before he awoke? The most she could do was hope. A tear trickled onto her cheek and she wiped the moisture onto her arm. Then she forced herself to pick up her bag and head down to the bar, closing the door behind her. At least she knew where to find him when she was ready.

SEEMS HE'D UNDERESTIMATED his Samantha. Mac knew the instant she left the room, and less than ten minutes later, he heard the slam of a door and the sound of an engine. He didn't need to glance out the window to know he'd see the red taillights of her replacement rental car peeling out of The Hungry Bear parking lot.

Letting her go was the hardest thing he'd ever done. But he had no right to hold her when she so obviously wanted to be gone. He swung his legs over the side of the bed and groaned. He'd banked on a couple of extra hours together. She'd bailed out early without saying goodbye. She was conflicted and confused, that much he understood.

He had only her parting whisper, words he wasn't meant to hear, to reassure him. "I love you, too, sweetheart." Mac said the words aloud for the first time.

He'd always thought the words would be the hard part. Never had he imagined the woman he wanted in his life would be elusive and hard to tie down. Whatever her reasons, Samantha deserved to do things on her own terms. Just as he'd decided to handle telling her the truth about him on his. Mac leaned over and reached for the phone.

AN OPEN-AIR LOBBY greeted Sam as she walked into The Resort. Plant life surrounded her, as did plush chairs and glass-top tables with Indian-drum-style bases. She placed her luggage down on the terra-cotta floor, allowing a bellman to take her bags. The hotel exuded warmth, tasteful decor, and as her fiancé had reminded her more than once, it came with a five-star rating.

"Can I help you?" A young clerk, a nice-looking man who couldn't have been more than twenty, greeted her with a smile. The eager look on his face reminded her of her own early days at her first job.

"My name's Samantha Reed. I'm with the financial conference that starts tomorrow morning." She glanced at her watch and cringed. "I realize my room probably won't be ready until much later, but I was hoping to at least store my things." She'd been in such a hurry to leave before Mac woke up that she'd forgotten she'd be temporarily homeless until a room became available.

Ignoring the pain in her chest that accompanied the mere thought of Mac, she focused on her empty stomach instead. "And I'm starving. Is there a restaurant where I could have breakfast and sit for a while?"

The young man glanced up from the computer and shot her a beaming smile. "Actually, we're all set up for you, Miss Reed. Your room is ready."

She blinked in surprise. "Must have been a slow week for you to have rooms ready this early."

"I, uh, yes. We had some early checkouts." He busied himself typing information into the computer.

She glanced around while she waited. The hotel sported a comfortable atmosphere in the beige, cocoa and white color scheme she'd described to Mac in her fantasy home. Their fantasy home, she thought, feeling the onset of tears.

Obviously she couldn't put her bartender behind her. Even this luxurious hotel reminded her of Mac.

"Miss Reed?" The clerk's voice grounded her thoughts. "If you'll just sign here…"

Sam scrawled her name and accepted her white coded key.

"Room 315A. Take those elevators in the corner and someone will be around shortly with your luggage." He pointed toward an alcove nestled between several shops. "The restaurant is down one level and is already open for business. If there's anything you need, don't hesitate to ask."

"Thanks again…" She leaned over the counter to read the name on his tag. "Joe. There is one more thing." She hated to ask, but she needed to know. "Has a Mr. Tom Webber checked in yet? Same conference."

The clerked tapped in a few computer keys. "Why, yes. Late last night. As a matter of fact, he left this for you."

A nervous fluttering arose in her stomach. "Thank

you." She looked down to see an invitation to a firm cocktail party late this afternoon and a handwritten note informing her he'd be by to pick her up fifteen minutes before. So they could arrive together, arm in arm. A command performance, part of her obligation as his soon-to-be wife. She'd have to get to Tom before the party or perform as planned and wait until afterward to talk to him. The thought made her ill.

She glanced at her watch. It was too early to awaken her fiancé no matter how much she wanted this trauma behind her. Well, she could take care of other things in the meantime. At least her father was an early riser, and he deserved to hear her decision before Tom called him, raving about broken deals and dire consequences.

As she headed for the bank of elevators in the corner, she wondered if Tom might accept things better than she anticipated. Perhaps he'd made idle threats to her father, ones he'd never meant to carry out. He'd seen a man weaker than himself and preyed on that weakness. It didn't mean he'd follow through.

Tom was a nice-looking man, more than capable of attracting women. This wasn't a love match, and there were plenty of women more beautiful than she was, women more willing and better suited to play the role of a rich man's wife. Not that she believed anything could salvage her position in Tom's company. He was ruthless in business, and his personal life would be no different. To save his ego, Tom would never keep her around. To save her sanity and find the life that suited her best, Sam would give her notice regardless.

Her room was at the end of a very long, elegant corridor. Light wooden hand-carved sconces lined the walls and lit the way. If she understood the signs correctly, this floor would be on the pool level, but her room was in the opposite direction.

Without warning, the rooms became farther apart until there were no consecutive doors anymore. When she reached room 315A, she discovered there was also a 315B. Connecting rooms, she assumed, and her stomach cramped in a tight knot.

She hoped Tom hadn't gotten any crazy ideas about spending any intimate time with his fiancée. Until now he'd been content with holding hands in public for appearance's sake. She hoped that hadn't changed. It would only complicate what had to be done.

She inserted the card key and opened the door to her room. Suite, she mentally corrected herself as she took in the spacious area that defined the word *luxury.* Not one amenity was missing. She stood in an oversize room with a kitchen in one corner and living area in another. Her sweeping gaze caught a plush couch, tables, telephone, VCR and large-screen television. A person could live here well beyond one weekend and never want for a thing. There had to be a mistake. She should have realized it the minute the clerk told her there was a room available on an early weekday morning.

Curiosity took over, and she decided to explore before reporting the error. One partially open door led to a bathroom. She peeked inside. Taupe-and-cream marble, not the standard ceramic usually found in hotels, covered the floors, vanities and Jacuzzi tub. She glanced upward, seeing the full-service shower massage with nozzles everywhere, even in the marble walls.

Wow. She and Mac would have a blast in a place like this. Imagine all the uses he would find for the myriad jets in the Jacuzzi and stall shower. Heat blasted her body as she recalled their first time together in the old tub over the bar. She wrapped her arms around her, but it wasn't the same. She missed him already.

The extravagance here was impressive, but she'd been happier at Bear's. Because Mac had been with her. This suite and its luxuries meant nothing to her without him.

Finishing her brief tour, she noticed two more unopened doors. One she assumed would lead to a bedroom, the other possibly to her fiancé. She shivered at the thought. No noises sounded from either room. If Tom were inside, at least he was still asleep.

Sam quietly picked up the phone and called the front desk, explaining her predicament to Joe.

"I assure you there's been no error, Miss Reed."

"I've been to many conferences, Joe, and I can assure you my company doesn't splurge on suites for its employees." A standard room would be more likely.

"Let me check." Sam heard the clicking of computer keys before the clerk came back on the line. "Well, you're right."

"I knew it."

"You've been upgraded."

"Courtesy of?" she asked, but she already knew the answer. And she refused to remain here and be obligated to Tom when she knew she was about to break off their engagement.

"Hang on a minute, let me check."

Sam drummed her fingernails against the glass tabletop. As things stood now, she'd have to pay for her expenses out of her own pocket, and she certainly couldn't afford to splurge on a suite. She'd have to budget carefully until she found a new job, and she didn't want to dip into her small savings unless absolutely necessary.

What kind of financial planner would she be if she didn't heed the advice she gave her own clients? Save and prepare for the future had always been her mantra. Too bad her dad hadn't listened. Then she wouldn't be in this predicament now.

Wrong. If she'd asserted herself from the beginning, if she'd taken control of the situation another way, she wouldn't be in this predicament now. She refused to blame her parent because she'd succumbed to old habits, agreeing to play the dutiful daughter out of a sense of misplaced need. Part of her new outlook meant taking responsibility for her role in this mess.

"Miss Reed? This upgrade's on the house," Joe informed her.

"Are you sure? But why…"

"I'm sorry, but I've got to run. An emergency, you understand. If you have any questions, just stop by the front desk later." A click was followed by a dial tone.

She'd been disconnected. "Five-star service my…" At least she knew Tom wasn't lurking in the next room. She slammed down the receiver. Loud.

If her accommodations weren't thanks to Tom, then whom? An even better question would be why?

A knock on the door interrupted her thoughts. "Valet," a voice called.

Great. Now her luggage would be deposited in this room, making it even more difficult for her to leave. She accepted her bags and tipped the bellman, then she called down to the front desk one more time. Joe insisted things were in order, refused to listen to her arguments and claimed there were no other available single rooms.

Sam tossed her arms in the air. "What else can go wrong?"

She tried her father, got his answering machine and left a message asking him to get back to her later. Ignoring the early hour, she called the hotel operator and asked to be connected with Tom Webber's room. His personal voice mail, another amenity of this lovely hotel, informed her he had an early teetime and lunch with clients, but he would meet up with everyone at the reception this evening.

She raised her gaze heavenward. "I had to ask?" Lowering herself onto the small couch, she propped her feet up and sighed. Confession was postponed, and all attempts at room switches would have to be done in person.

She had a day to kill. A day she could have spent with Mac, if she hadn't been so darn stubborn, so... The phone rang, cutting her off. "Hello?"

"Hi there, Sammy Jo."

Her heart began a rhythmic pounding that echoed in her ears. "Mac? Is that you?" Stupid question, but she was so relieved to hear from him she could have cried.

"Anyone else call you Sammy Jo...besides Zee, and he's outside waxing my car with no access to a phone."

"Waxing your... He's eighty years old. Do you want to give the man heatstroke?"

"I'm joking, Samantha."

"Oh." She laughed, even as she swiped at a stray

tear that trickled down her cheek. "But I'm not. No one calls me Sammy Jo but you."

"Damn right," he muttered. "And don't you forget it."

He wasn't angry. She would have heard it in his voice. At least she thought she would have, but she couldn't be sure. "Mac?"

"What is it, sweetheart?"

"I…I'm glad you called." She paused, listening to his steady breathing, letting the sound burrow into her heart and reassure her. "And I'm sorry I walked out on you this morning. But I have things I need to take care of here, and I didn't know how to say goodbye, and now I'm sorry because we would have had more time, and I don't know if you're angry. Of course you have every right to be, but…"

"You're rambling," he interrupted her.

She grinned, pictured him grinning back, and the tightness in her chest eased for the first time since she'd left him in bed. "I know."

"Because you're nervous."

"Yes."

"I can take care of that, you know." His husky tone caused every nerve ending in her body to quiver. He aroused her with innuendo, relaxed her with his voice and touched her with a simple phone call.

She squeezed the receiver in her hand. "How?"

"Trust me, sweetheart."

"I DO."

The simple admission did Mac in. He eased himself back against the pillow, wishing he weren't alone, that he didn't have to settle for her voice over the phone.

But the bar needed work, and Mac wasn't one to turn the reins over until the place had been cleaned up. He wouldn't ask Zee to help out, either. The old man had planned his weekly trip to the cemetery to visit his wife's grave. Mac couldn't intrude on his solitude. So until Bear returned in a few hours, Mac was on his own.

Think resourceful, Mackenzie. "Okay, sweetheart. Relax and tell me where you are."

She sighed. "My room."

He laughed. "I know that. I called you, remember? Describe it."

"Well, there's been some sort of mistake, and right now I'm in a suite. It's incredible. The colors, they're like a dream. My dream, the one I told you about, remember?"

As if he could forget. A house, a home, children, his and hers. Samantha's soft voice drifted over him like a cloud. She was happy in his hotel, in the suite that adjoined his, the one his sister used to live in before she got married and moved a few hours away.

"And Mac?"

"Yes?"

"You should see the bathroom. The colors are

heaven, and the tub? It's a Jacuzzi." She'd dropped her voice, and the husky sound brought him back to the moment he'd first seen her, dirty from the desert but irresistible, nonetheless.

"You know what else? It's got a shower massage." She paused a beat. "Hand-held, Mac."

He groaned. A pulsing began in his groin that only grew with each image she evoked. He'd pictured her in his tub, naked and relaxed, all soapy skin, legs spread wide...

"Are you there?" she asked.

He cleared his throat. "Yes. I thought I was the one that was supposed to be taking care of you."

"I thought we could take care of each other." The pause this time seemed less deliberate. "We were good at that, weren't we?" she finally asked.

"You know we were. Have you eaten yet this morning?" He grasped for everyday conversation. Safe conversation that led him away from thoughts of Samantha, shower massages and making love. Long distance didn't cut it.

A direct flight from Arizona to New York wouldn't cut it, either.

"No breakfast yet, but I'm *starving*." She let the word drawl out on her tongue in a way that shot his resolutions to hell and back. "What about you? Are you hungry?" she asked.

Ravenous, he thought, but not for food. He

glanced at the clock. A couple of hours more and this damn charade would be over with. "What are your plans?" he asked, steering her back to safe ground.

"Well, I have a cocktail party around four today, which is an obligatory thing, and then I've got... some personal business to take care of."

At which point he'd be back where he belonged and more in control of the situation. And himself. So far, he'd managed to keep the truth from Sam by offering Joe, his newest but most eager employee, a bonus if he managed to have Sam treated like a princess. One who had no idea who'd placed her on the throne.

That was Mac's job, one he planned on handling tonight.

"What about you?" she asked.

"I'll be doing my usual thing later on."

"Sounds good. Wish I could be there."

You will, sweetheart. You will. "I've got to clean things up around here...before Bear comes back."

"I never got to meet him."

Her wistful voice knocked a hole in his heart. "Maybe someday."

"Yeah. Maybe." Though he hated like hell leaving her with the impression that things between them were uncertain, she'd given him no choice. The telephone hadn't been invented for personal revelations this big. "Got to go, sweetheart."

"Bye, Mac."

He waited until she hung up the phone before doing the same. Then he dragged himself into the bathroom and turned the cold water on in the shower, full force. It would help ease the ache of desire, but not completely.

Only Samantha could do that. She had no idea what she did to him, and he wasn't talking just physically. Their relationship transcended sex. She taught him new things about himself, about his ability to love and give, but more important, she seemed to learn more about herself each day as well.

He finally had her where he wanted her, but the thought made him uneasy. As long as she remained in the dark, everything would be fine.

CHAPTER TEN

SAM BOLTED UPRIGHT IN BED. A sheen of perspiration covered her body, courtesy of the sensual dream she'd just experienced. Strategic parts of her body still tingled with the memory of Mac's hands on her skin, his lips tasting hers. She wrapped her arms around her waist to still the trembling, the yearning for something she couldn't have.

Because although Mac had called, he hadn't mentioned seeing her again. It hurt, she admitted, and she'd have to deal with that.

First she had to cope with reality, and that meant getting herself out of this gilded cage she couldn't afford. She swung her legs over the side of the bed and reached for her purse when she caught sight of her left hand and Mac's ring.

The ring she had to remove and replace with Tom's...at least until she officially ended things between them. Although she wanted nothing more than to keep Mac's ring close to her heart, she wouldn't humiliate her fiancé, despite his threats to do the same to her father. She might not love him, he might not love her, but they had an agreement. Once she'd said yes, he'd never been anything but accommodating and reasonable in their dealings. He deserved the same respect from her.

Her hands shook, and as she slipped the turquoise-and-silver ring off her finger, a premonition shook her, one similar to the eerie feeling she'd experienced in the tourist shop. *As long as you wear this ring, you will be wed for eternity.* Did that mean if she removed the ring, she'd break the spell?

"What spell?" Sam shook her head at her foolish musings. She'd never believed in such nonsense before and she refused to start now.

After carefully placing the special ring in her purse, she eased Tom's three-carat diamond attention-getter onto her finger. The gold band felt cold against her skin. Suppressing a shiver, she darted into the hall and shut her door behind her.

Back in the lobby, she waited until Joe finished with another couple before waving to capture his attention.

"Good afternoon, Miss Reed."

She smiled at the courteous young man. "Hello, Joe."

"What can I do for you?"

"Well, like I said on the phone, there's a problem with the room, I mean the suite."

"It's not to your liking?"

"I like it just fine, who wouldn't? It's just that I don't belong there. I don't know who authorized the upgrade, but it's a mistake. One I can't afford. So please check your computer and find me an ordinary, standard room."

He shook his head. "I already told you there aren't any other rooms available."

She wanted to scream in frustration. "You said this morning you had quite a few early checkouts."

"And just as many check-ins. If it makes you feel better, this one won't cost you…"

He must have caught her warning look because he stuttered before continuing. "This won't cost you more than the standard room you think you should have." He practically beamed again. "Satisfied?"

She slapped her hand on the desk. "Not by a long shot." But it wasn't Joe's fault. "I'm sorry. But please just put my name on a waiting list or something and let me know if an opening becomes available. Is that all right?"

"Yes, Miss Reed."

"Good."

His gaze had settled on her hand. Her left hand. "That's a lovely ring."

"Thank you," she murmured.

"I always knew Mr. Mackenzie had good taste. He's my idol, you know. I'd like to learn as much as I can about hotel management from him and then…"

Sam's brain screeched to a halt after his first few words. And she wasn't so certain she wanted it to click back into gear.

"Joe," she said, interrupting his running monologue.

"Yes?"

"You said Mr. Mackenzie." So what? Surely there were dozens of Mackenzies in Arizona. It was a big state. It didn't mean anything. "That wouldn't be Mr. Ryan Mackenzie, would it?"

He grinned. "Oh, he said you were sharp and had a great sense of humor. That's funny, Miss Reed. Of course it's Ryan Mackenzie. The boss said to take care of you until he got back, but he didn't say he'd be popping the question in the meantime. But look." He lifted her hand up to the light. "He most certainly has."

"The boss…as in manager?"

Joe blinked and didn't answer. Obviously he was unsure whether she was joking or whether he'd blundered. She had no desire to cause him problems, but she needed to know the truth.

She forced a grin. "Relax, Joe. I'm kidding. I know Mr. Mackenzie's status here as well as you."

His shoulders slumped in relief. "I knew that. I mean, I'm astute. I may never be an owner like him, I couldn't afford to purchase anything this grand, but I'll work my way up…."

Sam patted Joe's hand. "I'm sure you will." As soon as he learned the meaning of discretion and the value of silence.

A hollow, numbing feeling settled in her stomach. "About the room, I'll take it up with Mr. Mackenzie," she said woodenly before turning and walking away.

She made her way through the lobby in a haze of shock and disappointment. When she found an empty, oversize club chair, she settled in, curling her legs beneath her.

He'd lied. Her sexy bartender wasn't one. Oh, he was sexy all right, but he was no bartender. She wanted to be angry, furious and betrayed. And she was.

Even though that made her a hypocrite, because she'd done some omitting of her own during this week's retreat. She couldn't hold his lies against him, considering she'd wanted him to forgive hers. But she'd wanted him forever, while he'd wanted nothing of the sort.

His mistruths had a purpose, one that was now glaring and clear. This week had been a fantasy, nothing more. While she was giving herself to him, revealing a part of her nature she'd never shown another soul, a part she'd never known existed, he was withholding his true self.

While she was hoping and praying for a future, he was enjoying her newfound sexual freedom. The irony wasn't lost on her. Mac had gotten from this week everything she thought she'd wanted when she'd arrived.

And now? To Mac, the conference and her convenient stay at his hotel was probably a way to keep her around until she left for home. So he could continue enjoying their sexual exploits. She didn't want to believe it, but what else had this week been, but a festival of sex and sin?

Her heart begged her to be fair as a barrage of questions assaulted her. The emotions and feelings, could they really be all one-sided? And what about the ring, Sammy Jo? It figures that little voice would return now. Oh, Mac must have had a good laugh over the silver trinket she was afraid would bankrupt him. She'd been a cheap date, Sam thought wryly.

And what about his dreams and his revelations? The desire to build a house, the fantasy about children? "You said it yourself, Sammy Jo." He'd told her from the beginning they were indulging in their fantasies, and fantasies had a definite end.

When she left, he'd probably wave goodbye and say thanks for a good time. Why not? She'd provided one willingly.

Sam didn't know what hurt more, her stomach or her heart. Looks like she'd be ending her engagement but winding up alone after all.

She buried her face in her hands as the realization

washed over her. She'd gotten everything she came for. And not a damn thing more.

MAC STRODE THROUGH the lobby of his hotel. Knowing he couldn't risk running into Samantha, he'd showered, shaved and changed before leaving Bear's. Upon his arrival at The Resort, he tucked his bag away in his office closet, checked on his employees and made himself as scarce as possible.

Now a little before four in the afternoon, he needed to make sure things were on schedule. "Everything all set, Joe?" Mac leaned against the front desk in full view of the side elevators, so he could catch sight of Samantha before she could view him.

"Just like you instructed on the phone, Mr. Mackenzie."

After a week of being just Mac, he resisted the urge to look over his shoulder and see who else the young clerk could be referring to.

The name wasn't the only thing that felt strange. His clothes, a pair of black trousers, a white linen shirt and a sport jacket, standard for Resort clientele—hell, it was standard attire for him—felt stiff and awkward on his body.

Mac envied Bear and the relaxed comfort of his life. He never had before. Was it because his closest friend had found himself a soul mate, a woman who was willing to readjust her life and priorities in order to fit into his? Or was it because the time had come for Mac to stop living out of a hotel and move into a real home? A little of both, he assumed. He just couldn't be sure he'd end up with either.

But his friend had. Like Samantha, Bear's woman had merely been passing through his part of the world.

Impossibilities.

Improbabilities.

Bear would never desert Zee, just as Zee for all his zest and zeal, would never enjoy life outside of the Southwest. Which was why the old man didn't know all the details yet. It had taken some time, but Bear's lady, now his fiancée, understood that one of them had to sacrifice if they were to have a life together. Mac understood the same thing.

But with a hotel this size, his sister two hours away and his mother aging and incapable of handling responsibilities this huge, he couldn't be the one to give. That left Samantha, a woman with an older father and responsibilities of her own. Compromise, he reminded himself.

He turned to Joe. The guy had worked an extra shift and would be clocking out soon. "The flowers?" Mac asked.

"All set, sir."

Although he understood the necessity, the formality grated.

"The room will be filled as soon as she leaves for her cocktail hour," Joe said.

"The dinner?"

"Taken care of." If the clerk's smile grew any wider, his face would crack. Apparently pleasing the boss was high on his list.

"Champagne?"

"Done."

Mac had never been a hearts-and-flowers, romantic kind of guy. He still wasn't, and based on what he knew of Samantha, all he needed to do was explain why he'd neglected to tell her the truth. He didn't need to impress her with his wealth and surround her with luxury.

He might not need to do those things, but he wanted to. More than anything, he wanted to take care of her, to know she was safe in his suite of rooms and that she was his to come home to every night. He wanted her to know she was loved.

Because she didn't expect anything from him, he wanted to give her all that he had. And if he had to be honest with himself, he couldn't help think, courtesy of Zee, that some honest-to-goodness romance would smooth the way for the truth.

And a future. "The ring. Was it delivered?" Mac asked. He'd called in a favor and asked a good friend, a jeweler in town, to help him out.

"It's gorgeous. Fits her like she was born to wear

it. If I do say so myself, you have exquisite taste, Mr. Mackenzie."

He'd been referring to the one he expected to be delivered, not the one currently on Samantha's finger. "Maybe the extra shift was one too many, Joe." Or the kid was a bigger kiss-up than Mac had originally thought. Although his enthusiasm and hard work were commendable, he often went overboard. If Joe thought he could butter Mac up by gushing over the turquoise-and-silver ring, he had a lot more to learn.

Not that Mac didn't love Sam's ring and all it represented. He did. But this kid wouldn't know that. "I'll check in with Jim myself," Mac muttered. If his friend said the package would be here, it would. Still it couldn't hurt to check.

After all, what was a marriage proposal without a diamond ring?

"Uh, Mr. Mackenzie?"

"Yes?"

"Miss Reed at one o'clock." The kid nodded toward the front desk. He'd been watching too many James Bond movies, Mac thought, but at least one of them had remained alert.

Mac had nearly been caught unaware, and he moved to the side of check-in behind a marble pillar. Too much hinged on tonight's surprise to blow things now. His location hid him well. He had a clear view of the front desk and of Samantha as she approached.

His first look stunned him. He should have been prepared. He'd known, or at least sensed, what kind of world she came from. Even so, the woman approaching the desk didn't resemble his Samantha. After a week of seeing her, sometimes in short skirts, other times in a casual dress that hugged her curves, and more often than not, stark naked, her outfit now was something of a shock.

Sure, the silk dress clung to her breasts and accentuated her hips and curves, but it covered much more than it revealed with its high collar and long sleeves. Her dark hair, in stark contrast to the cream-colored silk, had been pulled on top of her head with a few stray strands brushing her shoulders.

She appeared regal, cool and aloof, all words he'd used regarding other women who frequented this hotel, but none he'd ever thought to use about the woman who'd spent the week in his bed. Until now. Mac would bet The Resort she wasn't wearing sexy lace underwear beneath that dress.

"Excuse me."

A deep male voice sounded from behind her as an older man came up by her side. Mac drew the line at eavesdropping and snooping even in his own hotel, but he couldn't leave without calling attention to himself, so he waited.

"Yes, sir?" Joe asked.

"My fiancée is expecting a call from her father.

Please have her paged at the cocktail party in the Western Ballroom if the call comes through."

"My pleasure, sir."

Mac stifled a chuckle. At least Joe kissed up to the guests, as well.

"And your fiancée's name?"

The man laughed, a rumble from deep in his throat. "Why, this young lady here," he said with pride.

Mac expected him to pull a woman from behind him. Instead he reached for Samantha's hand and rested their hands on the counter.

Mac's gut twisted painfully. He'd been in barroom fights in his youth, but this punch to his stomach was much more brutal and infinitely more severe.

"But…but…" Joe stuttered and shot his boss a confused look. Mac placed his fingers over his lips, indicating the clerk shouldn't give him away, and nodded that Joe should go along. After all, the older man knew what he was talking about.

His Samantha had an extremely large diamond on the third finger of her left hand. The same finger that had once held Mac's silver ring. The *token* of his affection. *Token* being the operative word.

What did she need with his tin ring when she had that huge bauble hidden away? For that matter, what did she need with a penniless worker when she had a rich man waiting? He now understood why she'd dodged personal questions and avoided his attempts to get closer.

Mac studied the other man, wishing he could criticize, but the guy was well-dressed and not the pot-bellied aging gigolo he often saw with the younger women here. The only thing Mac could jump on was age, which brought one of two choices to mind.

Had Samantha amused herself with Mac, the bartender, enjoying a fun-filled week of sex before settling down with the rich but older catch? Or had she pegged Ryan Mackenzie within minutes of entering The Hungry Bear and set her sights on his wealth immediately? Lord knows Zee had a big-enough mouth, and Mac hadn't exactly sworn the older man to secrecy.

He didn't know which possibility was worse.

They started to walk away when Samantha turned back to the desk. "Joe?"

"Yes, Miss Reed?"

"Has Mr. Mackenzie returned yet?"

The younger man opened and closed his mouth while Mac held his breath until Joe responded, "No, not yet." The kid just earned himself a raise, Mac thought.

"Thank you," she murmured.

Watching the couple walk away, he clenched his hands into tight fists. He had his answer.

The past week came back to him in flashes of truth. She'd come to him that first night in the store-room and played up to him until he'd asked her to stay. She hadn't jumped right into his bed, but teased and flirted until his control hung by a thread. The sex had been incredible, beyond his wildest imaginings. Yet his every attempt at emotional intimacy was met by her turning his attention back to their physical relationship. Even on the day they'd shared their dreams, she'd tried to pull away. Yet she'd finally bared her soul. Or so he'd thought.

But a woman who knew all along she was engaged to another man wasn't capable of sharing anything. Least of all her heart. She'd merely seen Mac as a better prospect and had gone after it.

Why marry a staid, conservative...dull type if she had a raging inferno waiting for her instead? Hell, the passion and fire between them burned so strong it nearly consumed them both, Mac couldn't deny that truth. He doubted Samantha could, either. So she'd told him what he wanted to hear. "I love you," being the words he had in mind.

If she'd been after sex alone, she wouldn't have whispered those three little words before her abrupt departure. But a woman with an agenda, one who'd strung him along, who'd whetted his appetite and curiosity from day one, who'd fed him every fantasy he wanted to hear... That woman probably sensed he was awake and whispered sweet nothings in his ear, wanting him to react accordingly.

And he had.

He ignored his thudding heart. He ignored the warning words in his brain telling him something was wrong. That his Samantha didn't have it in her to lead him on, to hurt him on purpose. Because despite all he'd viewed in the years since opening The Resort, he'd fallen for the very act he'd tried so hard to avoid.

Samantha epitomized every woman who walked into this hotel. The only difference was her ability to fool him. He didn't want to believe, but he couldn't discount what he'd seen. Mac had twenty-twenty vision.

He also had no trouble hearing, and she'd asked for him by name. She knew. For how long?

"Joe?"

"Yes, sir?" The kid looked as if he wanted to back off and comfort him all at the same time. The thought made Mac want to throw up. It also made him mad as hell. He didn't need anyone's sympathy.

"In your dealings with Sam…Ms. Reed, did you happen to discuss this hotel?"

The clerk paused in thought. "Yes, sir."

Hope sprang to life inside him. "And you told her I owned the place?"

Joe frowned. "Let me think. No, sir. She joked a little and I wasn't sure whether I'd blown things at first, but I believe her exact words were, I know Mr. Mackenzie's status here as well as you."

"I see." And he did, only too well.

"Should I...um, cancel your plans?"

"No." Mac slapped his hand on the desk. "Leave everything as is." Why go to the trouble of changing things now?

To think he'd spent a week feeling guilty when his lie of omission paled in comparison to Samantha's. No, he wouldn't change his plans. He wanted the satisfaction of seeing her face when she walked into a room full of flowers.

He wanted her to think she'd gotten everything she'd calculated and planned for.

And most of all, he wanted to see her expression when he yanked everything out from under her.

Because only then would she know how it felt to be taken for a soaring ride and then dropped hard to the ground. And because one small part of his heart wanted to hear her explanation. Even though it wouldn't make a damn bit of difference.

HER FEET ACHED from standing in pumps that weren't made for the shape of the human foot. As soon as Sam made it to her room, these shoes were going in the trash. So was this outfit that looked like she'd rifled through her mother's closet, playing dress up.

Which in a sense she had. Tom preferred she dress classy and sedate. Though he liked his women young and beautiful, he appreciated presentation. He wanted other men to envy him, not because he'd picked up someone who dressed to attract attention, but because he'd chosen the finest. Beauty speaks for itself, he'd said, and half her wardrobe had been acquired in the last six months to accommodate him and fulfill her end of the bargain.

Which had finally come to an end.

She stepped off the elevator and pulled her cream-colored pumps, bought to match her cream-colored dress, off her feet. Padding down the hall in stocking feet felt nothing short of heaven. Similar to the way she'd felt leaving Tom behind in the hotel bar.

She'd wanted privacy. He'd preferred the bar. She'd explained what she had to say was better done in private. He'd insisted she looked too beautiful to waste on an empty room. Finally Sam had given in and found a corner where they could be alone. She couldn't help it if he insisted on being dumped in public.

He'd taken the news gracefully. She knew he would. Tom was nothing if not civilized, and he'd never make a scene. But he had quietly reminded her that her father's reputation was on the line. To which she'd just as quietly asked him why he needed to pay for a wife when other women would line up to do the honors. The thought had silenced him for a while, and Sam could only hope he'd keep quiet at the country club regarding her father's financial state. Which, as Tom also reminded her, wouldn't be improving any time soon. No installments of money would be forthcoming to pay his debts.

She'd known that as well, and thanks to her dad's phone call earlier, he did, too. She'd been paged and had rushed to a private pay phone to return the call. Funny, but her father had sounded almost relieved. Maybe she'd underestimated him. She'd promised him they'd find a different solution and they'd talk when she got home, but her father hadn't hung up without telling her he loved her. A swell of emotion clogged her throat on hearing those words. She didn't have to sacrifice her life to gain his love.

Old patterns, Sam thought. He'd cajoled her into marriage and she'd agreed without fuss. He must have known she would. He also must have sensed her unhappiness. She should have taken control and ended things sooner. Everyone would have been better off.

Except that she'd have never met Mac. Never enjoyed this once-in-a-lifetime week. Though she wouldn't have her happily ever after, she'd treasure the time they'd shared. But she still had to face him once more. He'd lied and so had she. Sam couldn't plan the rest of her life without confronting the man she loved.

And she did have a life to plan since Tom's parting shot left her immediately unemployed. Also not a surprise. She'd reached her room, and she was dying to change out of this awful dress. Grabbing her shoes with one hand, she opened her door with the other. The suite was dark except for a dim light shining in the bedroom. She didn't remember turning the lamps off in the sitting area, but maybe housekeeping had been in.

She dropped her pumps and made her way through the dark suite toward the bedroom, unzipping the back of her dress and shimmying out of it as she walked. The silk pooled at her feet and she kicked it aside. Freedom had never felt so good. As she reached the bedroom, she hit the light switch on the wall.

The sound of a sharply drawn breath startled her and she whirled around, belatedly realizing she had nothing on her to use against an intruder.

"Damned if I didn't underestimate you again." She thought he muttered something about underwear, but she couldn't be sure.

"Mac." She exhaled a sigh of relief. At the sight of him, she forgot everything except her racing, pounding heart and the sheer joy of being in the same room with him again. She started a forward leap into his arms, but the hard look on his face stopped her midstride.

Suddenly she felt vulnerable and alone, two things she'd never felt with him before, and she wrapped her arms around herself to cover what little she could.

"You were expecting someone else?" he asked.

She studied his face, puzzled by the harsh tone, and said the first thing that came to mind. "You shaved."

He raised a hand to where his mustache had been. "I had my reasons."

"I see." She didn't. Not at all, but a sense of foreboding chilled her. She didn't recognize the stranger now standing in front of her. And the lack of a mustache wasn't the only thing that separated him from the bartender she'd known.

But she hadn't really known him, that little voice in her head reminded her. His masculine scent was the same, so was the effect it had on her body. Sex, she told herself, was apparently all that they'd had.

Her thudding heart made that statement a lie.

Reaching out, he toyed with the lace strap of her bra, his fingers idly playing with the material while his calloused hands whispered along her skin. She trembled beneath his touch, but his hands felt as cold as his voice had sounded.

"I thought maybe the sexy lingerie, the underwear that doesn't cover a thing, the tousled hair falling over your shoulders…was in preparation."

"For?"

"A seduction. You're good at that." His darkened eyes told her he remembered, too. But he played with her and she didn't appreciate the game.

"Of whom?" she snapped.

"That's what I'd like to know." Releasing her bra strap, he walked toward the window that overlooked the patio of greenery she'd admired earlier in the day.

As she watched him go, she looked around her for the first time. Multicolored bouquets with flowers she couldn't name decorated the room along with matching balloons in reds, pinks, whites and a variety of other shades. Her heart kicked into high gear, and hope blossomed like the flowers surrounding her.

She felt light-headed and dizzy. On the edge of a precipice, on the verge of getting all she wanted. Maybe. Was he upset she hadn't noticed his romantic efforts? Embarrassed he'd gone to the trouble? Maybe this was his way of apologizing for misleading her, and if so, she'd forgive readily. Once she leveled with him, perhaps they could start over.

She hoped with all her heart they could begin anew.

Ignoring her near-naked state—she'd stopped being embarrassed around him sometime after the first couple of incidents—she walked to where he stood and touched the rigid line of his back. "Mac."

He stiffened further.

"I'm sorry I didn't notice sooner. I had a lot on my mind, but...it's so beautiful. And you did all this for me?"

"Yes."

"Thank you." She wrapped her arms around his

waist, feeling the ripple of muscles against her skin for a brief second before he jerked away.

"Don't," he muttered.

"I don't understand." Fear slowly replaced hope.

"No, I don't suppose you would. I bought this for you, too." Turning, he opened a small jeweler's box.

A large diamond ring glistened brightly against the black velvet lining. "Mac, it's beautiful…."

"And even larger than this." He pulled her hand roughly out in front of her. Her silver-and-turquoise ring hovered between them.

She met his gaze. Confusion sparked his eyes, then dark anger followed.

Not understanding his reaction, she glanced down at his ring. She'd put it back on as soon as she'd left the bar. She'd wanted something of the Mac she'd known, even if he had turned out to be someone different than the man she'd believed him to be. "I love this ring," she said. "I thought you did, too." She lifted her gaze back to his.

"You're good, Sammy Jo. Better than I even imagined." He snapped the box closed and shoved it into his front pants pocket. "Tell me something. Would you have said yes?"

"Of course, but…"

"Of course. One question, then. What would you have done with fiancé number one?"

CHAPTER ELEVEN

HER LEGS WENT WEAK, and Sam lowered herself into the nearest chair. She twisted her fingers together as she started to speak. "I wanted to tell you. I was planning on telling you tonight, after..." Needing to gather her thoughts, she let her voice trail off.

"After...?" he prompted.

"After I ended things with Tom, and I did. Just now in the lounge. It's over, not that it ever was anything to begin with, but it was...necessary."

"And now it's not."

"No."

Mac stormed over to where she sat, bracing his arms on either side of the chair. A vein throbbed in his temple, and she noticed the tight clench of his jaw. Sam had never seen him this angry, not even when the guy in the bar had attempted to maul her in public. She swallowed hard, afraid that by waiting this long, she'd passed the point of no return. That he wouldn't listen to her explanation.

But he'd omitted things, too, so he should understand. "I should have told you, but Tom…the engagement is no longer necessary because…"

"I'm rich, too," he spat. "And with me, you not only get the money, but you get someone close to your own age and fantastic sex, as well. Well, good for you, Sammy Jo. You nearly pulled it off." He slowly clapped his hands in applause.

Sam stared in shock and dismay. Each word hit her like an arrow to her heart. The pain was raw and acute. Then as the ugly reality of his words sunk in, furious anger followed. How could he think so little of her when she'd given more of herself to him than anyone on this earth? Especially when he'd been less than honest himself.

She met his gaze, expecting the steely anger she'd seen earlier. It wasn't there. In his dark eyes, Sam saw a pain that mirrored her own. Gut-wrenching, real pain, and she grabbed on to it like a lifeline, because if he hurt, he still cared.

She reached for him, but he yanked his hand away. She tried hard to mask how that one gesture hurt. "You honestly think I knew you owned this place? From the beginning?"

He nodded. "Or close to it."

"You think I'm capable of that kind of deceit?"

He pinned her with a cutting glare. Point for him, Sam thought. She had deceived him from day one.

He'd done the same but seemed to have forgotten that fact.

"I'm sure Zee or one of the boys meant well when they told you," he said.

She folded her arms over her chest. "Loyalty doesn't mean anything to you, does it, Mac? Zee treats you like a son, but you think he'd betray you. And after what we shared…" She poked him in the chest hard. "You think I'd do the same. Guess we didn't share anything so great."

She forced the words past her lips, even as the pain shot straight to her heart. "We couldn't have, considering *both* of us were lying the whole time."

She broke into a cold sweat. Suddenly afraid she would faint and humiliate herself in front of him, she headed for the closet. She needed something to cover herself so she didn't feel so raw and exposed. Something to stop the chills that had taken hold would help, too.

His words followed her into the other room. "I overestimated your business ability, Samantha. You should never have walked away from one offer until the other was on the table."

Without waiting to grab the robe, she ran for the other room. "You arrogant, obnoxious, self-righteous…"

"Good choice of words, but if I were you, I'd

spend my time trying to catch your first choice before he finds a replacement."

"Maybe I…" The rest of her words were lost as the suite door slammed shut behind him. "Will," she muttered, knowing she'd do no such thing.

Sam didn't wait. With the slamming sound of the door still ringing in her ears, she darted for the bathroom, then the closet, and began tossing the few things she'd unpacked into her suitcase. She couldn't stay here. Not when the man she loved thought she'd…she'd… *Sell herself to the richest bidder.*

Oh, God, that's exactly what she'd been about to do. Until she'd come to her senses. Until Mac had taught her… What? About love?

She laughed until real tears began streaming down her face. She wondered if they'd ever stop. She might have fallen in love with him, but he'd had nothing more than fantastic sex with her. That much he'd admitted aloud.

The zipper got stuck on her garment bag and she tugged until it shut tight. Without pause, she yanked the carry-on off the bed and headed for the door. She flung it open wide, then slammed it closed again.

Where did she think she was going stark naked except for her underwear? She sank to the floor in a heap, luggage at her feet.

Stop and think, Sammy Jo. "And stop using that

ridiculous name," she muttered aloud. She had to get away from Mac and out of his hotel.

As she dressed, she admitted the obvious. "It's over." The pain was almost blinding. Clothed now in jeans and a T-shirt, she glanced around the suite one last time. To make sure she hadn't forgotten anything, not because she wanted to memorize the sweet-smelling flowers or the room-service cart in the corner with champagne chilling in a silver bucket.

But she'd never forget the warmth and flow of this room as she'd first seen it. She plucked a red rose from beside the trays of food. Planning to leave it on the pillow, she walked into the bedroom.

Then she remembered the ring. It was a symbol that spoke volumes, as did the effort that went into creating this setting.

"Oh, God." Sam closed her eyes. All that came to mind was Mac and the pain she'd glimpsed in his dark eyes.

He wasn't a vindictive man. She knew that. He hadn't gone to all this trouble after learning of her engagement, he'd done it before. He'd bought her a diamond ring and set the stage for a romantic proposal. Then he'd learned the truth.

She'd hurt him and he'd lashed out, hoping to hurt her in return. And he had. She pressed her fists into her cramping stomach. Oh, how he had.

Despite his harsh words, she understood. Not that understanding could change anything. When two people came together with lies as the foundation of their relationship, they didn't stand a chance.

She swiped at a stray tear. At least she'd leave with the knowledge she had meant more to him than a temporary fling, even if he no longer believed that himself.

Grabbing a hotel pad, she scrawled a note to Mac, then rolled the sheet and placed the paper and the red rose against the white pillow.

Maybe one day he'd look back on this week with pleasure and not bitterness. Love and not pain.

Maybe one day, she would, too.

MAC SLID INTO ONE of the many empty bar stools at The Hungry Bear. He studied the multicolored bottles of liquor lining the racks along the wall and wondered which would make him numb the quickest.

"A shot of tequila ought to kill the pain."

At the sound of the familiar voice, Mac glanced over to see Zee making his way from the storeroom in the back. "Where's Bear?"

"Where do you think? Setting his new family up at my place. The upstairs apartment is too small for Bear's rowdy boys and soon-to-be newlyweds. You didn't tell me I'd be having grandbabies so soon." The older man beamed with excitement.

Mac shrugged. "I promised."

"So you're good for something after all. Bear will be back to open for business tonight." Zee turned his back and began working on pouring them drinks, then slid the tequila Mac's way. "Here. You look like you could use this."

"Damn straight," Mac muttered.

"If you hurt Sammy Jo, I'll rip your heart out where you sit."

Mac rolled his eyes. Zee had only known the woman for a week and already he loved her. Unfortunately for Mac, he understood the feeling all too well.

Zee leaned across the bar. "Don't go making faces at me. She's a good girl who deserves better than to be lied to."

"Oh, really." Mac swallowed a harsh laugh, then reached for the salt and performed Zee's nightly ritual. Expecting the bitter taste of hard liquor, he nearly choked on the glass of amber-colored water.

"Shoe's not so funny when it's on the other foot, is it?" the older man asked.

"You knew?"

"I may be old, but I'm no fool. And you don't need to get drunk, you need to talk or you wouldn't be here."

Why argue the point, Mac thought. "What would you say if I told you Sammy Jo had a rich fiancé waiting back at The Resort?"

Zee didn't flinch. "I'd say there was an explanation."

Mac grunted.

"So what was it?" Zee asked.

"What was what?"

"Don't play dumb with me. What was her explanation?"

Mac shrugged, feeling like a teenager who'd knocked up a neighborhood girl and now had to face the consequences. "I didn't stick around to hear it."

Zee rounded the bar and smacked him in the head. "That was because your daddy's not here to do it himself," he muttered. Then he perched himself on a neighboring stool. "Usually when someone lies, they have good reason. You tell her you own The Resort yet?"

Trust Zee to get to the heart of the matter, Mac thought. And wasn't that why he'd come here in the first place? He looked at the man he thought of as a father. "She already knew."

Mac didn't need to ask the old man whether he'd been the one to inform Samantha. Contrary to what she believed, Mac understood loyalty. He knew Zee hadn't betrayed him.

Just as he'd known the minute he slammed the door behind Samantha he'd overreacted. But it wasn't every day a guy saw the woman he wanted forever with another man's ring on her finger.

Considering Mac had planned her ultimate fantasy—the fairy-tale proposal and the happily ever after—then to discover the truth the way he had was humiliating in the extreme.

"And you think she set you up," Zee said.

"No." Mac spoke emphatically. "Not anymore." When he first heard the news, he'd reacted with his heart and not his head. Now, having had time to think, he knew better. Hadn't he lied, too? Yet he hadn't given an inch when dealing with Samantha.

"But you thought so at first." They both knew the unspoken answer to that question. "Just don't tell me you told her."

"Fine. I won't tell you, so pour me a damn drink. Real liquor or I'm not having this conversation." Because although he'd felt like a fool, he'd acted like a jackass. He'd damn near called the woman he loved a whore. How the hell could he live with that?

Accepting the glass, Mac swallowed what looked like whiskey in one gulp. The raw liquid burned on its way down. "Good choice," he muttered. "Now keep them coming." Because only then could he forget the shock and the pain that flashed across her face with each cutting word he'd spoken.

"You had your reasons. Don't you suppose she had hers?"

Reaching for the bottle, Mac poured another shot glass full and drank before answering. "I'm sure she did."

"And the signs must have been there all along."

"That she was trying not to get too close? Yes. That she belonged to another man? Hell, no."

"Then focus on those reasons. And you can't do that if I let you get stinking drunk." Zee grabbed the bottle and shoved it beneath the bar. "Consider it payback for the watered-down crap you and Bear make me drink every night." He turned and headed for the back.

"Where are you going?" Mac hadn't come here to be left by himself.

"I figure if I leave you alone with yourself for company, you'll get smart and go after her." With that parting shot, Zee rounded the corner and disappeared.

Mac knew without being told that he'd been wrong. He knew his Samantha could not deliberately set out to entrap and hurt him. She just didn't have it in her.

"Think explanations," Zee called from the back room. "And then get the hell out of here."

Explanations. The woman had arrived straight out of the desert. What else did he know? She came from back East and had violet eyes he could drown in. Her mother died three years ago and she rambled when she was nervous. She was a financial planner and made love like she couldn't get enough of him. Her only family was an aging father whose love she sought, who was in debt up to his...

That was it. The father who needed money. What was it Samantha had said about the engagement? *Not that it ever was anything to begin with, but it was...necessary.*

And Zee was right. There had been signs. She'd promised her dying mother she'd take care of her father. *"Besides, I've always done the right thing."* And because she wanted them to love her.

"Dammit." She was marrying the rich old man to help out her father. Mac was sure of it. He was also sure she hadn't baited him to take the first guy's place. She'd gathered her courage and turned her back on her father's predicament and her word even when she'd believed him nothing more than a bartender. He may not know who told her, but he had a damn good idea of when she'd learned the news. And it was sometime after she'd left him at Bear's.

Mac knew this because he knew Samantha. Too bad he realized it so late.

"Good going, Mackenzie," he muttered. She'd spent the week breaking with old habits and insecurities. Hadn't he sensed the contradictions and watched her grow more confident with him and with herself? And just when she'd needed him the most, he'd hit her with lack of faith and trust. He'd rewarded her courage with accusations to burn her ears and singe her heart. She'd been searching for love and he'd probably convinced her she'd never have his. He'd acted low enough to lose her for good.

Mac muttered a curse and headed for his car, making it back to The Resort in record time. He had to find Samantha. Sucking up was the least he could do.

He didn't know where they could go from there. Hell, after his performance, he didn't know if there was anywhere to go, but at least he'd see her one more time. Now that the blinding rage had passed and understanding had taken its place, Mac needed that most of all.

When he reached the suite of rooms, he didn't knock, just inserted the card in the door and walked inside.

Honey, I'm home didn't seem like an appropriate line, so he just called her name. "Sam?"

Silence.

He knew she was gone.

A call to the front desk confirmed she'd checked out. He'd stood in this very room, had everything he wanted in his grasp, and he'd thrown it all away. His head started to pound, and he walked into the bedroom and sat down on the bed. His own stupidity overwhelmed him. If his accusations weren't enough, he'd gone and told Samantha to go back to her first choice.

Her parting shot came back to him with gut-wrenching clarity. *"Maybe I..."* Mac hadn't stuck around, but he knew how that particular phrase ended. Which meant she might still be in the hotel with the other guy.

He reached for the phone and realized that Joe, the only other person who could identify the fiancé, had clocked out for the night. Mac's gaze lit on the pillow.

His stomach constricted as he reached for the note left for him beside the flower. *"Mac, I would have liked 'forever,' even in a little apartment over a bar."* She couldn't have been more clear. She loved the man she'd believed him to be, not The Resort owner and jackass he'd become.

"YOU DON'T LOOK WELL, Mr. Mackenzie. That is, I mean you look tired this morning."

Mac raised an eyebrow at his still-eager but now flustered employee. "Lack of sleep will do that to you, Joe." So will restless dreams and erotic memories, Mac thought.

"Oh."

"Have you seen the older guy from last night? The one with Ms. Reed?" Mac asked.

"This morning on the way to breakfast."

He waited. Joe remained silent. What a great time for the kid to clam up and speak only when spoken to. Mac would have to pry the information out of him. "And was he alone?"

"No, sir. He had a stunning young woman on his arm."

Stunning blonde? Stunning brunette? Stunning Samantha? What? Mac wanted to throttle him for learning discretion in such a short time.

"They're still in the dining room if you'd like to…er, check things out."

Mac walked away from Joe and toward the restaurant, his heart pounding hard in his chest. Before he could pass the hostess desk, a voice paged him over the loud speaker.

Mac picked up the nearest phone. "Mackenzie."

"Hi, Mac."

"What's up, Kate?" Even as Mac spoke to his sister, his gaze strayed toward the hallway. His sister was merely checking up on him since he'd cancelled their weekend plans, and Mac attempted to reassure her…in between keeping an eye out for Samantha and the other man.

Seconds after he hung up, he found what he was looking for. The guy was coming out of the restaurant with a stunning… Mac craned to catch a glimpse. When he did, his breath hissed out in a rush. A redhead. A gorgeous, young redhead was on his arm. Relief swelled inside him because it wasn't Samantha.

But that meant he had no idea where the hell she'd gone. Home, probably, not that he blamed her.

Mac made it back to the front desk in record time. For all its headaches, being the owner had its privileges. And as he pulled the weekend's reservation cards, he thanked his lucky stars for each and every one.

CHAPTER TWELVE

SAM SLID THE BOX of office supplies, reference manuals and desktop accessories into a corner of her apartment. At least with the conference still going on, she'd been able to pack up and get out of the office without another confrontation with Tom.

The sizzle and drip of the electric coffeemaker drew her attention, and she poured herself a steaming cup of caffeine. She'd need all the energy she could muster to make some decisions about her life, and she wanted to start tonight. She stared at the classified section of the paper, though she had little drive to search the New York ads. Her heart and her soul remained in Arizona. With Mac.

Despite their last meeting, everything she wanted and desired out of life came back to their week together. But she'd blown that by not being honest from the beginning, or at least as soon as she realized her true feelings. She wondered what difference her honesty would have made. When all was said and done, she hadn't known him at all.

Hadn't she? If she shut her eyes, she smelled his masculine scent, she felt his hands easing their way up her body, and she heard his sensual voice in her dreams. In the dead of night, she conjured up the deep sounds whispered between them as they'd made love. She'd known and loved him well. Which was why his accusations and harsh tone hurt so very much. She'd left, but getting on that plane had been the hardest thing she'd ever done.

The loud buzzer signaling a visitor startled her, and coffee sloshed over the rim of the cup and onto her white lacquered table. Without taking the time to look for a napkin, she jumped up to answer the call. It was probably her father. She'd made some suggestions, and he'd promised to consider the options she'd offered and come by to discuss them. The one thing Sam didn't want was to be out of work and living on her savings for too long. Not with her father's debts still outstanding.

She'd already put in some calls to headhunters in various states where she thought both she and her father could start over. She'd liked Arizona, maybe too much, considering, but she couldn't get on with her life if she was constantly worrying about running into Mac. Of course, it was a big state, but the memories there would be overpowering.

She pressed the answer button that released the door latch downstairs and spoke into the intercom.

"Come on up, Dad." She unlatched the door, opened the lock and waited.

Two knocks sounded seconds later. "Don't be so formal," she called as the door slid open wide.

"Hello, Sammy Jo."

At the sound of that deep voice, her heart slammed against her chest and she glanced up. Since she wasn't asleep and couldn't be dreaming, that had to be Mac standing in the small entryway, and oh, was he a welcome sight. Dressed in tan slacks and a white linen collared shirt, he was imposing, refined and still an extremely sexy man.

She might be so happy to see him she wanted to jump into his arms, but his very appearance reminded her why she had to keep her distance. He wasn't *her* Mac. The man standing in her doorway seemed as out of place in her casual apartment as he was in her life.

She didn't recognize him dressed like this, but wasn't that the point? What did she know of Ryan Mackenzie, The Resort owner?

"How did you find me?" she asked. *What are you doing here?* would have made her seem too eager. Sam just wasn't sure she was ready to lay her heart out for him to trample again.

He shrugged. "Being an owner has its advantages."

At her obviously confused expression, he grinned. "I checked your registration card at the hotel."

"I see. And you're here to...?"

"Explain."

Anger quickly followed, and she cocked her head to the side. "The way you let me explain?"

He winced. "Maybe I deserve that, but I didn't come all this way to be turned away, Sammy Jo."

The sound of his voice caused a yearning deep inside her soul. She'd probably hate herself later, but she asked, anyway. "Then what did you come for?"

"You." He stepped inside. He stood so close, everything else faded. The blare of the car horns outside and the hum of her air-conditioning unit receded. His unique scent worked to heighten her awareness as well as her memories. "I made you a promise and I didn't keep it."

She recognized the husky undertones in his voice, and she struggled against the automatic arousal that swept through her body. "What promise was that?" she asked.

"I told you we'd use all twelve. We still have some left." He grinned, a charming smile meant to disarm her.

Unfortunately, they'd passed the point where sexual innuendo worked to lighten the tension. "Interesting you should pick that point, Mac. Seems I was right. Sex was about the only honest thing we shared. Everything else between us was a lie."

His hurt gaze cut deep. "You might have convinced yourself of that, but it isn't true."

"No? I don't even recognize you dressed like that." She fingered the collar of his expensive shirt. "And minus the mustache, I'm facing a stranger."

"External things, Sammy Jo. And just one damned convenient excuse so you can protect yourself from me." He circled her wrist with his fingers in a grip so gentle, the gesture caused tears to pool in her eyes. "You don't need to, you know."

Was he right? Was she protecting herself from this man who, until he'd uncovered her deception, had never done a thing but give her pleasure and make her happy? Yes. Because she was afraid. How did she know what had been real between them and what had been part of their fantasy? How did she distinguish between reality and the facades they'd presented in place of the truth?

He reached forward and tucked a strand of hair behind her ear, one that must have fallen out of her ponytail. His fingertips grazed her neck and she trembled, closing her eyes. The gesture gave Mac hope.

It had taken him more time than he'd wanted to arrange things at home, and three days had passed before he could arrive with the news he wanted to give her. Even if he didn't look like himself, he was still the same man she'd fallen in love with. He only hoped she'd realize that fact.

Nothing much he could do about the mustache

now. He'd taken one look in the mirror and remembered her words. *"Don't ever shave that mustache... At least not while I'm around."* Then he'd conjured her image, his Sammy Jo with another man and he'd reacted...to prove to himself she wouldn't be in his life anymore and to give himself some semblance of control, something he hadn't felt since she'd fallen into his arms at the bar.

"You came for me," she said at last, sounding surprised. Wide-eyed, she met his gaze.

Damn, but he loved this woman, and he owed her more than he'd given so far. When this was over, she'd never doubt him again. An explanation was the least he could give her. What happened afterward was her decision.

He lifted her hand, drawing her fingers through his. "The Resort started out as a small bed-and-breakfast," he said slowly.

"Really?"

He nodded. "It was my father's, along with acres and acres of surrounding land. The Resort was like a dream of his. Only, thanks to a heart attack, he didn't live to see it. We grew up comfortable." Needing to touch her, he kept their hands entwined, his thumb drawing lazy circles around her palm. "The money came later, when I sold some of the land to build the hotel and turned it into something big. Of course, the times and the economy had a lot to do with its success."

"I'm sure you're being modest, just as I'm sure your father would have been proud."

"Of the business, yes. Of how I paraded around flaunting my newfound wealth? No." He wasn't thrilled with himself and his behavior in the earlier years. It was humiliating how fast he'd taken to money and how quickly he'd forgotten his roots.

She remained silent so he continued. "I had only myself to blame when women guests started throwing themselves at me, and I guess it went to my head. By the time I realized it wasn't me they liked but my status and money, the damage had been done."

Clear, curious eyes met his. "Who hurt you, Mac?"

"That's the strange part. No one woman in particular. No one meant enough to me." *Until you.* He pressed a kiss against the top of her hand. "It was the life and the fact that these women were capable of carrying on an affair while their husbands were staying in the same hotel that turned my stomach. So when I met you and you liked me for who you thought I was, I didn't correct you. And by the time I needed to come clean, you had backed off emotionally."

She stood quietly, obviously respecting the way he needed to explain. But she pulled their hands against her cheek as she waited.

"I guess my views were jaded. I just didn't realize

how badly until I turned on you. You paid for something you hadn't done, Samantha." He untangled their hands and walked toward the window overlooking a park, putting space and emotional distance between them. He'd had his say. The rest was up to her.

Like the first time, she had to come to him.

SAM WATCHED HIM STARE out the window and beyond, to the grassy park below. Mac was wrong. He wasn't the only one to blame. She'd been selfish and unfair. By coming to him with an agenda, she'd set him up without knowing the background and baggage he'd brought with him to this relationship.

And yes, they'd had a relationship. Despite what she'd told him, she hadn't been able to convince herself steamy sex was all she and Mac had shared.

She paused a few feet behind where he stood. He'd managed what she thought was impossible; he'd diminished the anger and hurt. Instead she felt even more love for this special man.

"I'm equally to blame, Mac."

He turned and faced her, leaning against the window.

She swallowed hard. "And seeing as how I understand better now, I guess that absolves you, too." She shifted from foot to foot.

"So now what, Sammy Jo?" The distance between them couldn't be more than four feet, but to Sam, it felt like a chasm the size of the Grand Canyon. This wasn't like them. She and Mac had always shared a remarkable comfort factor she'd never felt with anyone else.

He'd come this far for her. She had to go the rest of the way. Honesty, she reminded herself. The very thing they'd lacked until now was the one thing that could bring them back to each other.

She held out her arms. "You could lose the distance between us," she whispered. If he'd just hold her, she would know everything was okay. The words would follow.

He looked at her, his dark eyes more serious than she'd ever seen them. "One question."

She pulled her arms back to her chest, her hands curling into fists. Her nails dug into her skin. "Yes?"

"Do you trust me?" A question they'd asked each other many times over the course of the week together. Never had it held so much meaning.

She knew what he was really wondering. Did she trust him despite the lies and omissions, despite the horrible things he'd said and implied, despite the reality of who they really were?

None of it changed what mattered most. What they meant to each other. "Do I trust you?" She repeated the question aloud. "With my life."

The second Mac had his answer, he held out his arms and she jumped forward, plowing into him full-force. She didn't know who was more relieved, Mac or herself, when she was finally back where she belonged. His deep, heartfelt groan told her he felt it, too.

This was right.

They were right.

Needing to taste him, she sealed her lips against his and kissed him with an urgency she'd never felt before.

He broke the kiss first. "Does this mean you've forgiven me?" he asked, moments later.

She tipped her head back and looked into his dark eyes. "I think we both needed forgiving."

"Meaning our lies canceled each other out?" he asked wryly.

She shook her head. "They weren't lies, they were omissions."

"That took on a life of their own because of how we felt about each other."

Drawing on every bit of reserve strength, she met his steady gaze. "And how is that?" she asked. Because for all they'd shared, not once had the words been spoken.

"I love you." His words wrapped around her heart and filled every empty space inside. "I do, Sammy Jo. And if that means shelling out money to get your father back on his feet, I will."

"My father..."

"The reason you'd marry a man you don't love."

"How did you know?"

He grinned. "Easy, sweetheart. I know you." He grasped her hand and twisted the ring she still wore on her third finger. His ring. "It just took me time to get over the shock and start thinking like a rational human being."

"Thank you," she whispered. Considering his views on women and his wealth, this offer proved how very much he loved her. "But Dad and I have come to an understanding. I had him checked by a doctor, and physically, he's fine. He realizes the extent of what he's done and is ready to get back on his feet."

"Sounds like you've covered a lot of ground in a short time," Mac said.

"Thanks to you. You made me see I couldn't give up my life for him…and once I met you, I didn't want to."

"I can help your father pay off his debts, if you'll let me."

She shook her head.

"You're not saying no because you're afraid I'll think you're after my money."

"I'm saying no because our life, our love has nothing to do with his problems. But for the record, I'm not looking for a hand on your wallet."

"No?"

She shook her head once more. "But I can think of plenty of other places I'd like to put my hands." She grinned as she reached for the zipper on his pants. "For the record, Mac, I know you, too."

"You do."

Samantha nodded. "I was wrong to think I didn't," she murmured, kissing his lips, his face and neck. The rasp of his zipper being lowered resounded in the small room.

Mac suppressed a shudder as desire ripped through him.

"It isn't what you're wearing that matters. It's what's inside the clothes that counts." And apparently she wanted to get there as soon as possible. She yanked on his pants and he helped her get them around his legs and into a pile on the floor.

Her gaze fell on his erection, and her hands quickly followed the direction of her stare. She gripped his hardness between her soft fingers. "No underwear," she said with a grin. "I like it."

He let out a harsh groan. They'd have plenty of time for foreplay. The rest of their lives, if Mac had his say, but right now he needed to be inside her.

Reaching beneath the short denim skirt, he found her skimpy underwear. "About as much as I love the fact that you wear these things," he muttered. "Because they're so damn easy to get rid of." With one jerk of his hand, he ripped the silk garment off her body.

"Wow." Her eyes opened wide.

"You think that was good?"

"Impressive."

"Considering I'm a nice guy, or does that label no longer apply?"

She touched her face to his, aligning her cheek against his more-roughened skin. "You're still a nice guy, Mac."

"You said you'd have liked forever, even in a small apartment over a bar. What about in that fantasy house you described? Would you move to Arizona, Sam? I spent the last few days pulling together a list of firms who would be more than happy to have your talent on board. And I know some people who could help your father start over. What do you say?" he asked, holding his breath.

Her soft moan nearly undid him. Then her words did. "That's a yes, in case you weren't sure."

Lifting her by the waist, he held her at the tip of his erection. In one easy stroke, he slid himself inside her.

Sam moaned as they joined together at last. Her moist and wet body accepted him like he belonged to her. Because he did. She exhaled at the ecstasy she'd found with her bartender that wasn't.

"Look at me," he said.

She stared into his charcoal eyes, darkened by passion and other more complex emotions she could now let herself name.

"For the record, Sammy Jo, this has nothing to do with sex and everything to do with love." He jerked his hips upward, fitting himself deeper inside her.

"I know." She swallowed an unladylike moan of passion. "But you can't deny that the sex is incredible."

He grinned. "I never did."

"And for the record, Mac, I love you, too."